Friday night had arrived, and Vicki cou~~ld not wait to start getting ready~~ .er night out with Amber in 'Malibu' the local nightclub. The excitement had begun earlier in the afternoon as Vicki and Amber began the dubious task of getting themselves dance ready. It involved Amber coming to Vicki's house to decide what was going to be worn, doing their hair and make-up, whilst enjoying a few small ciders along the way. Vicki always begun by doing her 'tan' which was somewhat a dangerous task, as it usually ended up on the bedding and everywhere else it shouldn't be, but she loved a bit of colour and would never dream of being seen with 'white legs'. "Amber, pass me the baby wipes again, will you please? "asked Vicki, as she leant across her bed trying hard not to touch anything. She was waiting on her "golden tan" drying, but she had noticed the palms of her hands were looking as though they had been dipped in brown varnish. Eventually, Vicki had successfully scrubbed the fake tan from her palms and felt it was safe to move again, having ensured she was dry and looking as though she had just come off the plane from Alicante. "Looking good babes.... That 'Sun In 'you used earlier has really lightened your hair as well, you look as though you've have been away on your hols..." remarked Amber, as she stood backcombing her hair to the heaven's in front of the bedroom mirror, then dousing it in copious amounts of hairspray, so that it wouldn't collapse.

"Got a good feeling about tonight Amber, think we might be lucky and if not, we have always got a Kebab and "The Hitman & Her '' to look forward to ", they both burst out laughing at Vicki's optimistic outlook and continued to dress to impress. "WOW! that Rara skirt really goes with that crop top Amber...you look as though you've jumped off the pages of 'Vogue' magazine." exclaimed Vicki, much to Amber's delight. Amber struck a pose and began swinging her Rara skirt from side to side, "I love that skirt on you Vicki it sure shows off your tan, here's hoping no-one spills a drink down your legs and you end up all streaky..." chuckled Amber, as the two girls finished their ciders.

"Think that's your taxi here love ...." called Vicki's Mum from the living room, where she was sat enjoying her weekly fix of 'Dallas'. Vicki often wondered if her Mum would ever leave the telly behind and go out herself, she might meet someone to keep her company rather than the TV. Then again, her Mum seemed content watching her shows, but Vicki did worry she would get lonely once she moved out into her own place. James and John were away living their own lives now, it was only Mum and herself, here in the same house where she had grown up and experienced some good and some awful things. However, tonight was going to be enjoyable ...well as enjoyable as a night out in Hollowburn could be! "Bye Mum!

Don't wait up!" Vicki called, as she and Amber ran out the front door to the taxi, leaving behind the overpowering smells of 'Samsara' perfume and 'Aqua Net' hairspray lingering throughout the house.

Waiting patiently at the bar, Vicki casually glanced right then left along the length of the busy bar checking to see if there was any good- looking talent in tonight worth bothering about. "*Mmmm...one or two maybes...*" she thought to herself, before being brought back into the room. "What can I get you? "asked the thin, greasy looking barman directly at her, "Can I have 2 ciders and blackcurrant please?" She replied, struggling, trying to get to her purse, which as per usual, always ended up at the bottom of her handbag, just when she needed it. Eventually, after what felt like forever, she found her purse and paid for the two drinks, then began making her way carefully back across to Amber, so that no drinks would spill onto her tan.

It was Friday night in 'Malibu' the only decent place to go in Hollowburn to drink, dance and hopefully find a good- looking lumber at the end of the night. The place was right in the centre of town which was good for getting home, otherwise, Vicki and her friends liked to go up the Town to Glasgow, where a good night was always guaranteed, mostly because guys came from all over, and if you made a fool of yourself on a night out, it was fine, because the chances of meeting the people again were minimal. Whereas, here in Hollowburn everyone would soon know what you had been up to!

'Malibu 'on a Friday night was always better than a Saturday, Vicki and her friends had a theory; that this was due to guys being out with their friends on a Friday night, whereas the Saturday night was more couples, and this was when they usually discovered if the guy, they had met on the Friday actually had a girlfriend. This had happened once to Vicki and she vowed it would never happen again. The club was decorated in deep red velour trimmed off with silver around the seating areas and bars, even the hallway upstairs to the toilets had the same deep red carpet, which you could feel your feet stick to due to the drink spillages, the cigarette smell, just added to the atmosphere too. This didn't stop her going to the club, she found the build up to her nights out exciting. Vicki and her friends enjoyed the music which was played from Motown to chart stuff. She rarely left the dance floor once she was up. Vicki realised she always loved a Friday night out with her friends even as a teenager, however, now she was grown up and had a different group of friends.

"Hey... Vicki do you fancy a dance?" Vicki turned in the direction of the question, there in front of her stood Michael Gold. Vicki recognised him straight away, as he still had his strawberry blonde hair, although tonight it was slicked back and longer at the back, almost a mullet style. Michael offered his hand out towards Vicki and led her onto the dance floor the sound of 'We Don't have To Take Our

Clothes Off' by Jermaine Stewart, Vicki's favourite song at the moment. Once, on the dance floor the music took over and they both danced whilst checking each other out... Vicki liked Michael's shirt and leather jacket he was wearing but thought shoes would have been better than the Kickers he was wearing...BUT, "hey-ho", She thought to herself. he was looking good otherwise. Michael, meanwhile, could hardly hide his delight in the older Vicki dancing in front of him, he felt lucky that she had accepted to dance with him, found himself smiling, hoping he could remain in her company once the song was over, as he had always fancied Vicki but was not sure whether she knew or not. On the last note of the song Vicki turned to walk back to where Amber was sitting waiting, watching their drinks and handbags, unaware that Michael was right behind her following in her direction.

As Vicki sat down. she could smell Michael's aftershave, as he shimmied up on the seat next to her. "So ... What have you been doing since I last saw you Vicki? "he asked in her ear, the music was thumping loudly around them. "Mmm... Well, I still live at home with my Mum, although I am hoping to move out if I get promoted in my job." Vicki thought this sounded grown up, "Are you working? "Michael asked, as he leant closer towards Vicki. she could feel her heart thumping and hoped he couldn't. "At the moment I'm a trainee journalist for a regional newspaper, but hopefully won't be long until I'm a fully- fledged journalist, I'm always on the lookout for that one exclusive story, which will set me on my way up the ladder", she chuckled, thinking this was quite cute and would make Michael see her as the career woman she wished she was. "That's a good job Vicki, hopefully you will get your big break soon, what about Carol....do you still see her?" Vicki always dreaded answering this question.

Everyone that Vicki knew Carol knew, the fact that they were best friends, or had been best friends. Most of Hollowburn was aware of the horror in which both girls had been involved in their teenage years, and unfortunately some folk still lived with the nightmare daily. Fortunately, Vicki realised she was more resilient that most folks and was trying to move forward with her life, the determination she had shown in her youth was going to ensure she had a good future and life to look forward to.

"Sadly, no I don't see or hear from Carol at all nowadays Michael, we kind of fell apart about a year after all the Jonjo stuff. Carol found it hard to move from the past, her anxieties have ended up ruling her life ". Vicki never got used to saying that she and Carol were no longer friends. She felt a deep regret that some things just could not be put back together, especially when it was your best friend. However, Vicki went onto explain to Michael that she had tried hard to help Carol through as much as she could, but that Carol did not want to help herself at that time and she had changed personality wise too. Vicki had always loved the way in which Carol could always see the good and be positive about people and situations, however, events had turned her into a totally different person. The days Vicki had spent with Carol after the Jonjo O'Neil murders were tough for them both. They had witnessed the brutal killing of Father Mulhern and the devastation that had left behind. Vicki and Carol dealt with the aftermath in totally different ways. Vicki talked through her emotions with her family and a counsellor, whereas, Carol locked herself away in her bedroom and would not talk to anyone about her feelings, not even her big Sister Tracy, whom she admired. Vicki spent days and nights trying to encourage Carol to get out and about again, but she sunk deeper and deeper into a depression. Carol became withdrawn and her personality became bitter and twisted, the total opposite of the way she used to be. Vicki eventually had to move on for her own sanity, but she had not fallen out with Carol they simply grew apart!

Checking her watch, Vicki realised that the club would be closing soon and could not believe how time had flown in Michael's company. It seemed they had a lot in common and shared the same dreams and ambitions for the future. Vicki silently wished the night could go on forever, then the club beat slowed down, as the last dance came on. Michael stood up and Vicki's heart sunk as she thought he was going home now, but as he stood in front of her he put his hand out, gesturing towards the dance floor...Oh how Vicki's stomach was doing somersaults, butterflies, whatever they were called, she felt giddy with excitement, she was floating, as she went onto the floor as George Michael sang ' Careless Whisper ' she snuggled into Michael's neck as he held her tightly .

CHAPTER TWO

Sitting at her desk on Monday morning, staring at the typewriter in front of her she thought about her weekend and meeting up with Michael after all this time. It was amazing, how well they had gotten on, when he eventually kissed her at the end of the night, she hadn't wanted the kiss to end, never mind the night. He had the softest lips, she didn't mind the fact that her favourite Twilight Teaser lippy would be shared. They had exchanged telephone numbers, Michael had promised to call during the week to arrange a date, she could hardly contain herself and was having problems concentrating today.

"VICKIII …" came the holler from her Editors office across the hallway. Looking up, she could see Dougie Thompson standing at the side of his desk, waving a white sheet of paper about in the air, all the while staring in her direction. "Jeezo...what now" she whispered under her breathe, as she made her way into the office. "Have you heard about this Vicki?" passing the sheets of paper to her. Vicki read the headline, '20th Century Slavery ', emblazoned across the top. As she read the story, it became apparent that there had been girls found in a house in the Elton Estate, which was in the next town to Hollowburn. Vicki read in disbelief, as it unfolded that the girls were living in fear for their lives, after been given the promise of a new life here in Scotland, they were actually trafficked and being used as sex slaves. This story gave Vicki chills up and down her spine. The Elton Estate was made up of six blocks of maisonette type flats and was known as the place where most of the unsavoury people lived. The Estate was well rundown with most of the windows having plywood instead of curtains. "This is terrible Dougie... How can this be happening and right on our doorstep?" Vicki felt the adrenalin course through her body, she decided this was going to be her big break, the one she had been waiting on. Now, she only had to convince her Editor that she could do something with this information, make him and herself proud, as well as helping these poor vulnerable girls.

"Let me work on this Dougie...I can do this!" she enthused, slamming the paper onto his desk. "Please," she added quickly, as she saw him rubbing the back of his head, a recognised sign he was thinking. "I will not let you or the paper down...I promise you, just this one chance to prove myself that I can be a good investigative journalist ". She stopped there, as she knew pleading was not a good look for anyone, never less a serious journalist. "Right...let's see what you're made of Miss Carey, DO NOT let me down and...please STAY SAFE!" came the words, she thought she'd never hear. "YES!" Vicki exclaimed, turning, she marched with her head held high from the office, determination written all over her face.

CHAPTER THREE

Carol Walker hated her life!

"Another day, another dollar" whispered Carol to herself, as she checked the lights for the sixth time and walked towards her front door. This was slowly becoming her new mantra, helping her get up and out the door in the mornings. The fact that she checked and double checked, plugs, sockets and windows, before attempting to leave her flat had become 'normal' behaviour to her, she thought nothing of it, as much part of her daily routine as brushing her teeth now! Carol knew deep down that it was not 'normal' and did have moments of clarity whilst actioning these practises, that this was anxieties from her past, which she had pushed away to the back of her head, if only she had the courage to face them, she knew she would be helping herself and her family.

Carol lived alone, in a third-floor flat on the Elton Estate. The Estate was on the outskirts of the town and housed a mixture of elderly, families and singletons. The majority of flats were in a state of disarray, if truth be told, needed pulling down and rebuilt again. However, everyone knew this was not going to happen anytime soon and some residents worked hard at trying to clean it up. Carol was not one of these residents, she liked to keep herself to herself. The quiet life was all Carol asked for nowadays, she wasn't interested in the goings on in and around her estate. In fact, she barely spoke to anyone apart from Mr Jones, the elderly man who lived next door to her flat. Carol knew what it felt like being the centre of attention and she had no need or desire to ever go back there!

The ghosts of her past were holding her back in her existence today. Often, she would look back at where it had all begun to go wrong for her and ask herself why she had become so involved, in something which really had nothing to do with her at all. If only she had been stronger in standing up to Vicki at the first mention of looking into Jonjo McNeil's murder and left it to the Police. Her life would probably be a whole lot better at present, if she had not been so easily influenced by her friend's desire to be, 'Cagney & Lacey ', at the time. Thinking back, they should have gone straight to the Police, at least the majority of problems they had caused, for themselves and others could have been minimal. The only consolation was that they had helped catch Jonjo's murderer and found Mary Donachies' long lost Son in the process. There were times when Carol wondered what had become of Mary and Peter

Donachie. The last she had heard they were moving out of Hollowburn, to a place where no-one knew them or their story. They were still visiting Mary's Son Charlie in prison, where he was serving 10years for the murder of Jonjo and Father Mulhern. It was said, that Mary could not go through the pain and heartbreak of losing another Son, she was going to be there for Charlie, since she felt so much guilt at missing out on such a large piece of his life already. Carol felt sorry for the woman, but more so for herself, as she felt she had paid a hefty price for assisting in this reunion of sorts, especially with the loss of her friendship with Vicki and her health. There were days when Carol felt quite upbeat and tried to be positive, but there were more days when she felt stressed and down in the dumps. Carol's Mum and Sister Tracey were forever on at her, to let go of the past and to move on with her life, because her Mum was always stating that she was merely existing, not living, which for a young woman was no way to carry on. No-one understood that she was trying to move on, but the nightmares still came every once in a while, and she would often wake startled, with sweat running from her, as the images of Father Mulhern's bruised and battered body, lay in front of her. It was moments like those, she wished she could forget everything, have some kind of life. Whilst the years had passed since she was an outgoing teenager, who had enjoyed her life, to an extent, she wished she could go back to being more like her old self. Outgoing and full of potential for a bright future with her best friend Vicki by her side, she didn't know it at the time, but she had everything, life was good, until they had got themselves so involved in someone else's business.

Today would be like every other day in Carol's life. Get up, wash and dress, grab something to eat then set off for work at the supermarket. This was not the kind of job or even life she had envisaged for herself, but she enjoyed the structure working gave to her. Working on the checkouts at the supermarket was mundane at times, but the day went in quickly, she liked the interactions between herself and customers, due to the fact it was only temporary contact and superficial. Carol got on well with her colleagues, but never allowed anyone close enough to really get to know her well. This suited her, she knew she could retreat at the end of her shifts to her sanctuary in the Elton Estate. Nowadays, she felt more in control of her anxiety, due to years of counselling and medication from her Doctor. It was something she dealt with on a daily basis, she was now at the stage where she would consider some days... good days. Living alone was testimony to all the hard work she had done on herself and when she allowed it, she would feel pleased at herself, this was the hope she was holding onto.

Walking towards the stairwell heading to work, Carol shook her head in disgust at the dog mess on the landing, and was trying to avoid stepping on it, when she heard a lot of shouting and swearing, coming from the flat opposite Mr Jones's. It sounded like a foreign man, shouting and threatening, whoever was in there with him. Carol closed her eyes, counted to ten and quickened up her pace as she hurried past, not wanting to get involved in whatever was going on, past experiences taught her well. *I'll really need to speak to the council about this place it's getting worse...* she spoke to herself, something she did all the time, when she began answering then she'd worry, she told herself with a small chuckle. Out on the street, Carol looked up as she heard the slamming of a door, she saw a white male with two young girls, they had just come from the noisy flat, she thought the girls looked scared, but pushed this to the back of her mind and thought about her day ahead instead.

CHAPTER FOUR

"Morning" sang Vicki, as she walked purposefully through the office to her desk. Since she had been given the greenlight with the suspected slavery lead, she felt energized and motivated. Getting dressed in the morning Vicki made a conscious effort to look professional. Today, she was wearing a new cream silk blouse, along with her grey cigarette trousers, with matching grey fitted jacket. In her hand she held her briefcase, which held a new Filofax, which her Mum had bought her, to celebrate this new story she was working on.

On the day, she had been given the go-ahead for the story, she had rushed home and found her Mum and Brother John in the living room chatting. Vicki's arrival made them both turn swiftly, as she exclaimed, "Well...say HELLO to The Daily's new investigative journalist!" she was beaming from ear to ear. "I would if I could meet whoever it is..." grinned John, as he got up and walked over to lift her up, twirling her around the living room, whilst her Mum clapped and laughed. It was no secret to anyone who knew Vicki that her dream job was to be a fully-fledged journalist.

As she made her way into the building, her mind was already focussed on the day ahead and how she was going to start investigating the allegations of slavery and corruption, which was going on in the Elton Estate....

The one thing she knew for certain, was that she needed to gain some useful contacts within the Police department and within the Estate itself. Sitting at her desk, Vicki began jotting down some notes from the information which she already had, then she remembered the young Police Officer who had helped Carol and herself after the Jonjo courtcase. "I wonder,I wonder...." She pondered loudly, "You wonder what?" quizzed Colin, her older colleague, who sat opposite her desk. Colin was an experienced journalist, as far as' The Daily 'went but she didn't trust him entirely, therefore she was coy in her reply, as she wanted to keep HER story close to her chest. Vicki knew Colin would try to sabotage her chance, if he thought she was onto something big. "Oh! nothing much Colin, just thinking out loud...." She replied, as she got up off her chair and made her way towards the exit.

Vicki set off in the direction of the local Police Station, she realised this may well be a long shot, but right now she had nothing substantial to go with and she thought nothing ventured nothing gained. There was more to be gained by asking her only Police contact than not asking, so she proceeded on her quest. The sun was shining, she was feeling positive, it was amazing how a little bit of sunshine made everyone feel better and happier, she certainly hoped this would be the case with the Officer; that he would be approachable.

Entering the Police Station, Vicki's heart began beating that bit faster, she was aware of the beads of sweat on her brow, *Oh my God....* She repeated under her breathe, to herself, *Get a grip!...* she was telling herself, as she took several deep breathes, trying hard to contain her composure. It had been during the Jonjo court case, when she had last stepped inside these walls, she thought she had overcome the past, but it was obvious at this moment in time, that the past emotions were still very raw. Inhaling deeply, she tried slowing down her breathing, straightened herself up and approached the desk where a Sergeant was standing, " Can I help you?" he enquired, looking straight at Vicki, she was certain he was staring at the sweat on her face, pushed this thought to the back of her mind, she replied, " Yes....I hope so, I am looking for an Officer Young... I'm not sure he's still stationed here?" She was informed that he was still working at the station and waited patiently, whilst the Desk Sergeant phoned the relevant department.

It felt like forever, but eventually she heard footsteps, looking up, to see Officer Young approach from behind the desk, he gave a small nod of recognition, "Hi I'm David Young... I believe you are asking for me?" he stated, as he looked her up and down. He was certainly a bit older looking now, but she recognised him and hoped he would remember her. "Hi! my name is Vicki Carey...we have met before...." She replied, as she shook his hand and gave him direct eye contact. Vicki had settled down, in the time she spent waiting for Officer Young to show, so she felt back in control of herself. She knew she would need to act like a professional, in order to gain respect from the Police Officer.

After a few minutes of re-establishing themselves with each other, Vicki explained the reason for her visit. Officer Young showed her the way into a small interview room off the main reception area of the Police Station and asked her to take a seat. As he closed the door behind him, he walked over to the opposite side of the table and sat down. "Right....so what do you have on the Elton Estate?" he enquired, rather smugly, thought Vicki. "Well... let's start the way we mean to go on here Officer" she was just beginning to say, as he interrupted her, "Let's start by you dropping the Officer, you can call me David... *Ohhh he's suave!* Vicki said to herself, *here he obviously thinks I have come with some big news...* she sniggered, slightly under her breathe. "Ok, David.... I've not came here today to report any crimes, I've came to see whether we can work together on finding out if there are any crimes, we can solve on the Elton Estate!" there she had said it. Now she was praying he wouldn't laugh at her and throw her out of the station. "So! what do YOU think is worth both of us spending our time looking at on the Elton Estate?" he replied cautiously, Vicki realised he was not going to make this easy for her, she would need to divulge some of her reasoning, after all it was she who was asking him for assistance in working together.

Once Vicki had explained her initial suspicions of the activities, which were going on in the Estate, David relaxed a little and sat back listening intently with the occasional nod of his head, as she made it clear she would not give up on the story, until she had stopped the abuse of the girls being kept there. He allowed Vicki to finish explaining her findings, then he agreed that they could work together, sharing some information, but he explained there was a Police protocol regards sensitive information. She would need to understand that he could not divulge this or be known to have divulged this! Vicki understood what he was saying, they agreed to keep this between the two of them, until such times, when they would require more Police involvement.

CHAPTER FIVE

Sitting at her checkout, scanning other people's groceries, Carol imagined the lives the people led back home. It was interesting she thought, the way in which people shopped. She could tell from their trolley, whether they had a partner or not, as the single folk usually couldn't be annoyed cooking a meal, therefore settling with a meal for one. Carol gave a big sigh... as she realised that was her! The store was unusually busy for a Wednesday, then she realised it was the end of the month, it was always busier then, as people bought their monthly shopping, hoping it would last them until the end of the next month. Carol's thoughts drifted back to her own Mum and how she would buy her shopping in on a daily basis, probably more expensive to do it this way, then again, her Mum didn't have the money for a big shop and lived from day to day back then. Carol could feel herself getting agitated, as the memories came flooding back to life when her Mum and Dad had lived together. It was a scary unsettling time in her life, with her Dad's need for the bottle and the affect it had on his behaviour. It was due to his drinking and abusive behaviour, which had led to her Mum being hospitalised several times, with one near death experience, finally bringing her Mum to her senses. Life had been testing back then, she knew in her heart that it was her friendship with Vicki Carey and her big Sister's strength and determination which had got her through. Carol quickly stopped herself from revisiting there and focussed on her conveyor belt and its contents again.

The first thing she noticed was the smell of 'Kavos' aftershave hitting her nostrils, *Jeezo, has this guy washed in this?* She thought to herself, the smell was so strong, she chuckled as she lifted her eyes and there he was...the epitome of tall, dark and handsome! Oh! MY! was he handsome! Standing there in front of her till, wearing a black leather jacket, jeans and a khaki t-shirt, he wore his dark hair gelled back and he had eyes so deep, Carol felt she could swim in them. Carol struggled to string her words together when their eyes met as she served him. This was a strange new feeling she was experiencing, she wasn't sure if she liked it or not, there was something familiar about this guy, she felt as though she had met him before, yet, she was certain she would have remembered. She watched him leave the store, hoping their paths would cross again soon, as she was struggling to get him out of her mind.

The bus was full, it was standing room only on the way home, Carol decided to jump off 4 stops before her own, as she hadn't seen Tracey or the kids for a few days, she popped into the corner shop at the bus stop to buy the kids their chocolate and sweets, which she knew were their favourites. She enjoyed seeing their smiles and spoiling them.

Tracey and the kids had moved closer to her and her Mum recently, after the break-up of her marriage to the kids Dad. Tracey was left with Timmy and Tommy, after their Dad had gone off with another woman, Tracey's then neighbour. Carol had always had reservations about Big Tommy but had put it down to her hatred of all men. This was extreme, but true since witnessing her own Dad battering her Mum and the constant shouting, she held sheer hatred for men. Tracey and her Mum tried tirelessly to tell her that not all men were like their Dad, but it fell on deaf ears, because Carol was not interested in men. until she thought of the 'Kavos' man at her till today... she would keep that to herself for the time being.

As she walked towards the door to Tracey's flat, she could hear the two boys playing and laughing, this made her heart burst, she smiled. Carol loved her nephews and her sister and would always be there for them, no matter what, because Tracey had always been there for her.

Tommy opened the door after one knock, the delight in his eyes was clear to see. Carol always joked she wasn't sure if it was due to seeing her or the fact, she always brought their sweets. It was a lovely warm greeting either way, she grabbed him into her arms for a big hug. When Timmy realised who was at the door, he ran at Carol, as she walked into the hallway. Tracey popped her head out of the kitchen door, "Cuppa Carol?" she asked her sister, Carol struggled to walk with her two nephews hanging onto her ankles, until she produced their sweets. "How was work today then? Busy? "asked Tracey, she could see Carol was in good spirits today, she wished she could be like this all the time, but she also understood the pressure Carol's anxieties placed on her, although she tried to push Carol into doing things which she thought would help her. "Yeah it was busy, end of the month madness..." Carol almost told her about 'Kavos' man, but she knew if she did Tracey would just go and on about him, anyway, she might never see him again. No, she'd keep him all to herself for now. Tracey made dinner for Carol and the boys, then they watched "Baywatch" before putting the boys to bed. When the boys were tucked up, Carol and Tracey opened a bottle of white wine and sat putting the world to rights, until Carol noticed the time, realising she had missed the last bus home, decided to stay the night at Tracey's.

The next morning Carol got up with the boys and made them all breakfast. Tracey had a lie in, she loved it when Carol stayed over, it was the only time she could get some time to herself, as the boys loved spending time with their Auntie. "Right Tracey, I'll need to go shortly, or I'll miss another bus!" Carol called along the hallway. Tracey appeared from her bedroom, dressed and ready to get the boys to school. "Can I borrow your deodorant please?" Carol asked her Sister, making her way into Tracey's bathroom, "Yeah help yourself, can't have you smelling out the store, now can we?"

Carol made it into work just in time to clock herself in, sometimes if she wasn't in on time her workmate Gayle would dock her card for her. Gayle was the closest person Carol would call a friend, although, she kept her at arms- length and on a need to know basis. Carol liked it this way! "OHHH just made it Missy, did you have a late night?" joked Gayle, she knew Carol never went anywhere or had any real friends to go anywhere with. "Stayed at Tracey's last night" she answered, walking to the office for their checkout cash drawers.

The constant sound of the till bleeping, the reoccurrence of scanning, small talk and giving change was mind numbing most days. Today, Carol was feeling optimistic and energised at the thought of maybe seeing 'Kavos' man again. Since setting eyes on him yesterday, she could not stop thinking about him, she had fallen asleep with grandiose ideas of them together. It was 20 minutes until her shift ended, when she caught a whiff of him. Sitting at her checkout, her heart began beating so loud, she was certain the customers she was serving could hear it, *Oh my God!* ...she was repeating, over and over, as she tried to remain calm, the aroma getting stronger, which she knew meant he was at her checkout and getting closer by the second. Scanning a ready meal for one and four bottles of beer, Carol looked up to find **HIM** standing, watching and smiling at her, looking as gorgeous, as he did the day before. *HE can hear my heart beat...*she was telling herself inwardly, absolutely mortified, she felt herself blushing. "Can you give me some change of a pound as well please?" he asked, the moment he spoke, and she heard his Irish accent, she realised exactly why she had felt that she knew him, and who was standing in front of her...Charlie Sweeney!

Shocked and temporarily speechless, she could only nod as she looked out the correct change. Handing it across to Charlie some of the silver fell onto the counter, both leaned across to retrieve the change, his hand caressed her arm, she could not contain herself any longer, "Charlie? Charlie Sweeney?" she exclaimed, much to his astonishment. "It is you... isn't it?" she repeated, over again. Charlie looked slightly amused, before replying to her, "That depends on who's asking Darling", the customers in the queue for her checkout decided to use other operators, as Charlie and Carol reacquainted themselves.

Leaving the building, she could smell that aftershave again, she was beginning to think she was imagining it, but then she saw Charlie, standing against the wall smoking a cigarette, looking like Danny Zuko, from the film Grease. Heart pounding again, she was trying her best to look calm and collected, but knew she was failing miserably, as she felt her cheeks hot, she could feel her palms wet and sticky with sweat." So! We meet again Miss Carol Walker...." He crooned, whilst stepping on the stub of his cigarette and making his way over towards her. Standing there in front of her, she took time taking him in. The years he had spent in jail had obviously been spent in the gym, as he looked muscular, this only added to the air of danger which he still held.

CHAPTER SIX

Weeks passed, Vicki felt that she was getting nowhere with her investigation into the abuse case. There had been one woman, who lived on the Elton Estate that had concerns, but she refused to say why, when Vicki had stopped her in the courtyard of the Estate. When Vicki had told Colin, she was going to knock on people's doors and ask them directly about any concerns, regarding crimes being committed on the estate, he laughed in her face. He told her she was mad to think anyone would place themselves in danger speaking to her. Vicki could see where he was coming from, and realised it was a basic way of investigating, however, she felt it was the only way she was going to find out what was going on.

Climbing the next flight of steps up onto the next landing, Vicki's optimism was slowly diminishing. Every door she had knocked on up until now was either unanswered, or if it was answered there was no knowledge of anything un-towards going on within the Estate. This didn't surprise her, she knew it was going to take someone extremely fed up and wanting action to speak out about the problems which were evident in this Estate, but the people here were too scared to speak out about them. Just as she had finished climbing the graffiti, urine smelling stairs, she turned onto the landing, she heard shouting coming from a few doors down, from where she stood.

Stopping in her tracks, Vicki steadied her breathing and stood against the wall, trying to hear what was going on. The shouting was coming from a male, she was certain it was being directed at a female. Apparently, he was angry because she had not done what she was meant to do and there was no money, which he had told her to bring back with her. At this point Vicki heard banging and screaming, which was clearly a female. Vicki could not believe what she was hearing, she felt unsure, as to what she should do. Standing listening to what she believed to be someone being beaten, she was scared and frustrated. Just as she had decided to go call for some help, the door opened, and two white males exited, slamming the door behind them.

Vicki watched as the two men walked in her direction with their heads down, they were in deep conversation with each other and did not look her way. Standing, she felt as though her feet were stuck to the spot with fear, heart beating, she tried to calm herself down to enable herself to take in some details about both men. It was clear they were not from around this area from their accents, one sounded Irish and the other possibly from Birmingham, she wasn't certain of that, but she'd go with that just now. The man doing most of the talking, was the Irish sounding one. He was tall with light blonde/ginger hair, some would call strawberry blonde, she guessed. He wore a trendy expensive looking bomber jacket with a t-shirt beneath and denims, she noticed he was wearing white Kickers on his feet, he was quite attractive she thought, but he had an air of danger around him too. The other guy was bald and slightly shorter in height, but bulkier in size, he looked as though he worked out in the gym a lot. His clothing wasn't as trendy or expensive looking and he wasn't as handsome, she guessed from the way they were interacting with each other that the Irish fella was in charge. Digging deep into her shoulder bag for her note pad, her mind trying to keep the picture of both men, she eventually found it, then noted down the descriptions, as best she could, so that she could share them later with David Young.

Placing her note pad back in her bag, Vicki then proceeded with caution along the landing, until she stopped outside the door of the flat from which she had heard the commotion. Unsure if she was doing the right thing or not, she decided against the small voice in her head, which was screaming at her to run from the building. Knocking on the door, she was terrified of it opening, and what she might find behind it, but the investigator in her, told her she was doing the right thing. This was the only lead she had found on this case, she felt this was going to be the start of something big she was onto. No-one answered the first few knocks, but she was determined she was not going to give up, as she knew for certain there was at least one person beyond that door.

"Hello... It's ok I know you're in there, I want to help you!" she called gently, through the opening of the letter box. No answer came, but she could hear whimpering inside...."Hi my names Vicki... if you open the door I can help you, I promise" she realised she was making a promise which she might need to break, but if it got the person to let her in , she would try her best to keep her word. As Vicki took a step back from the door, she heard footsteps from within coming towards the door. YES! ...she thought, *Keep coming...Come on, just open the bleeding door....* she was beginning to lose some patience, which wasn't her strong point at the best of times, she willed the person to open and let her in. After what felt like an eternity to her, she heard the door unlock, as it opened slowly, she let out a slight gasp, at the sight in front of her. Standing in front of her was a young girl, no older than thirteen, half dressed, covered in bruises with tears streaming down from her young face.

Vicki bent forward with her arms out to offer support to the girl, "I won't hurt you, I promise you, I'll try my best to help you, come with me...." She pleaded, as she offered the girl her hand. Much to her surprise, the young girl grasped her hand and leaped from the other side of the door onto the landing next to her. "Come on, let's get out of here!" she said, pulling the girl into her arms and escorting her towards the stairwell. They hurried across the estate, towards the main road, where she had parked her car away from the Estate. Vicki guided the girl towards her car, opened the door, settled her in the backseat, jumped into the driver's seat and set of in the direction of safety. The young girl was shaking with fear, tears continued to stream down her cheeks, they made their escape towards Vicki's office, it was the only place where she knew the girl would be safe, and it would allow her some time to get her own head together and think about her next plan of action.

Upon entering the office, Vicki was aware of the attention she was getting, as her colleagues watched with interest at the sight of herself, with the young scantily dressed and bruised female at her side. Vicki popped her head around the staff room, upon finding it empty, she asked the young girl to take a seat, whilst she went to speak to her Boss Dougie.

Having seen the commotion Vicki had caused by her entrance with the young girl, Dougie was already aware they had a visitor. "Who and What the hell is going on?" he asked her, as she entered his office. Vicki knew this was not an ideal situation she had placed everyone in, but she had no other choice, as she had to flee the Estate quickly, this was the safest option for her and the girl. "Please Boss, I didn't know what else to do or where to go" replied Vicki, as she walked towards the chair opposite Dougie. Sitting here in the safety of the office, with people around her, she felt calmer, allowing her thinking to become clearer. "I realise I should not have brought the girl here, but I panicked and did not know where else to go" she pleaded to her Boss's better nature, "She's been beaten by two fellas, she only looks about thirteen!" she continued. "Where did you find her?" he asked. Vicki proceeded to tell Dougie about her days activities and how she had come upon the young girl. Dougie could not believe the danger she had placed herself in, "Vicki, firstly there is no story worth placing your life in danger for!" he stated, he was shaking his head from side to side. "Anything could've happened to you! What, if they guys had taken you as well?" he went on, it was only now sitting here, that the enormity of the situation had finally hit her. "But I couldn't just walk away and leave her Boss, I had to get her away!" Vicki could feel herself getting emotional, whilst she stood up, she made her way out of the office, towards the staff room with Dougie following behind her.

On hearing the door open, the young girls head turned to face them, it was clear to see the fear in her eyes. Vicki walked over to where she sat and took her hand, as she sat down next to her. "Can you tell us your name please?" she spoke softly and calmly, all the while stroking the girls' hand gently. "Mandy" she whispered, "Hi Mandy, we won't let anything bad happen to you, no-one is going to hurt you" Vicki continued to try and reassure the girl, as the young girl stared with fright in Dougie's direction "How old are you? Your parents must be at their wits end with worry"

"I don't have any... I'm thirteen next month "Mandy said meekly, pulling herself back from Vicki, trying to fold herself into the corner of the sofa on which they sat. Dougie placed a glass of juice on the table next to the sofa, "Mandy Dear, how did you end up in that flat... with those men? Can you tell us?" he enquired gently. Vicki was surprised at how sensitive he was being to Mandy, she knew he was not happy about her being there. Mandy began crying again, "I don't want to talk about it" she sobbed and put the cushion up to hide her face. Vicki nodded her head towards the door, a signal for Dougie to leave the room, she followed behind him. Back in his office, they sat silently deep in thought, pondering how to move forward.

Due to Mandy being under sixteen and appearing to have no parental guidance as such to return her to, they decided the best thing for her would be to contact Social Services. Vicki realised that she would need to try to find out how Mandy had come to be in the flat, and get some information on the two guys, before Social Workers got involved, as she couldn't see them allowing her to talk to a journalist, once she was in their care. Entering the staff room, she gently closed the door, went over and sat next to where Mandy lay curled up on the sofa. "Hey Mandy...It's only me, can we talk please?" she caressed Mandy's arm, as she spoke. Mandy turned to face her, and Vicki noticed more bruising appearing on her face. "Mandy, where did you meet those two men that were in the flat with you? Do you know their names?" Mandy looked up, her bottom lip began trembling, as she told her, "They came up to me on the street and started talking to me, the Irish guy gave me some cigarettes and told me he would drop me off wherever I was going, so I went into the car... but they took me to that flat" she began to sob heavily. Vicki remained next to her, gently stroking her arm providing her with some reassurance. Mandy began to calm down and continued with her story, which Vicki was finding hard to listen to, as she calmly reassured her to help divulge all the gory details of her life up until that day.

Social Services arrived and after being filled in on the information which Mandy had divulged to them, she was taken to a safe place of care. As she was being escorted out the of the office area, Mandy came up to Vicki, wrapped her arms around her neck tightly and whispered, "Goodbye Vicki and thank you!" Vicki returned the hug, and reassured Mandy that she would be in touch soon. Afterwards

Dougie and Vicki digested the information, which Mandy had told them, deciding that they needed the assistance of the Police, with the knowledge which they had. This was something big and too dangerous for them, Vicki knew who to get in touch with.

CHAPTER SEVEN

Since meeting Charlie at the store, Carol's life had been turned upside down. Instead of spending her evenings alone watching tv, she was being taken out for dinner and drinks, at least four nights of the week. This was totally out of Carol's comfort zone, she was exhausted from all the effort it was taking keeping up with Charlie and his lifestyle. Carol was spending money, buying new outfits to wear for going out, this was money which she really could not afford to spend. The fact she was falling behind with her rent payments and other bills, she forced to the back of her mind. The anxiety which was once almost paralysing and affected her life on a large scale, seemed to be more controllable, she was certain this was due to Charlie's calming influences. Charlie was everything she thought he would be, charming and extremely attentive, he was always complimenting her by telling her how beautiful she was, he bought her flowers and presents, something which she was not used to. He made her feel safe and this brought on a sense of calm, which she kept telling herself was so odd, considering that he had done time for murder. Maybe, the fact that she felt he was not a complete stranger, had helped their relationship move at such a fast pace.

Carol was in her bedroom listening to the new Boyzone cassette, singing to herself, as she backcombed her hair to give it more height, she admired herself in the full-length mirror. The pink fluffy top she had bought yesterday looked good with her denim skirt and jacket along with the new silver stilettos, made her look taller and slimmer. Her favourite song 'No Matter What' was playing, she sang the words, whilst thinking about Charlie, the feelings she had for him were getting stronger and this frightened her a little, her stomach flipped when she thought of him and their times spent together. Charlie had waited until she felt ready to sleep with him, he did not push her into bed, she went willingly, he was far too sexy, she had wanted him as much as he had wanted her. The first time they had spent the night together, they had been out for dinner at the Italian restaurant in town. It had been a lovely evening, they had enjoyed flirting with each other across the table. At the end of the evening, he had walked her home to the Estate, she invited him in. Carol made coffee, as she brought the cups into the living room, Charlie had taken them from her hands, placed them onto the small table, took her hands and guided her onto the settee next to him. Carol's heart was beating so fast, her breathing quickening, as he kissed her softly, becoming more passionate, as he gently lay her back onto the settee, he was lying on top of her. Things heated up quickly, before she knew what was happening, they were removing clothes and making their way towards her bedroom. That night Carol experienced sensations she didn't even know she could feel, she hoped that she had pleased Charlie, enough to keep him interested in her. That was a few months back now, and their relationship was going from strength to strength.

Tonight, they were together in the pub sitting chatting happily, watching the people coming and going. Charlie was still fairly new to the area and did not have a lot of friends, well, that's what he told Carol. As he got up to go to the bar for another round of drinks, she dug in her bag for her lipstick and compact mirror, reapplying some to her lips. When she turned to see if Charlie had been served yet, she noticed him chatting to a tall strawberry blonde guy at the bar, it looked as though they were not strangers, just from the way in which they were talking and their body language. Minutes passed, Charlie was still in deep conversation with the guy, she thought about going up to introduce herself, to find out what was going on, she was beginning to feel ignored by Charlie, sitting here all by herself. Just as she was summoning up the courage to go introduce herself, Charlie turned from the bar with the two drinks in his hands and started walking in her direction. "Who was that you were chatting with?" she tried to sound casual, but even she could hear the irritation in her voice, she was never any good at hiding her feelings. Charlie placed the drinks on the table, sat down next to her, "Just some guy I used to know from way back" he replied, "Looked like you knew him well, from the way you were gabbing away there " she was trying to keep her cool, but she was failing miserably, she had a feeling there was more to Charlie and the guy than he was letting on, but decided to let it go, she could see something was bothering Charlie. The rest of the evening she spent trying to coax Charlie into conversation, as he was unusually quiet and at times seemed distant. At the end of the night he dropped her off at her door, said he had to get up early, so would just spend the night at his own place. Upon entering her flat on her own, Carol couldn't help but feel deflated, her anxieties began getting the better of her, she knew in her heart something wasn't right with Charlie, after he had met with that guy at the bar, she was beginning to worry that whatever it was, it was not going to be good for them.

Charlie was enjoying his time he spent with Carol, although they knew each other from way back, they never reminisced, mainly because it upset Carol, due to her fall out with Vicki, which pleased him, because he really wasn't interested in going back the way, he was only focussing on the future, and what he could gain from this latest venture he had found himself in. Since his time in jail, he had become close with his birth Mum Mary and her husband Peter. Charlie wasn't sure he wanted a relationship with Mary, after her placing him up for adoption, as a baby, but Mary was adamant that after everything which had happened, and her losing her other Son Gerrard so tragically, she was not going to allow this Son to walk away from her. Time and time again, she applied for a visitor's pass, he declined the request, until he had received a long letter from her, explaining her circumstances and reasons for placing him in adoption. Basically, she thought she was doing the best thing for her baby Son, she had no-one to help her and was too young to take care of a baby. Mary was not to know then that Charlie would grow up with all this resentment and anger, which had enabled him to be bribed by the Priest, causing so much harm and distress, to so many people, her Son and his half-brother included. Mary and Peter visited him on a regular basis when he was in prison, giving them plenty of time to talk openly about their true feelings towards each other, ironing out the issues which were there at the beginning. Nowadays, Charlie felt relatively comfortable when he was in Mary and Peter's company, he had even spent a few weeks staying with them, when he was released from prison, until he had found the flat, he was in at the moment. During this time, he enjoyed the fussing Mary made of him, making sure he had everything he needed, taking care of him, like a real Mum. It would break her heart, if he got himself into trouble again, he knew he had to keep this latest venture from her!

The first day he had seen Carol sitting bored at her checkout in 'Safeways', he had not realised who she was, more important to him was where she stayed. He needed to be able to keep an eye on his new business venture, without anyone realising he was involved. Meeting up with Carol would be the perfect cover, allowing him to watch whilst having some fun too. He had watched Carol for a few weeks, unbeknown to her, at first, he had not recognised her from his past in Hollowburn. It was during the days, as he followed her and overheard conversations with work colleagues that he had put two and two together and realised who she was. He knew he could use this to his advantage and began putting his plan into place. Carol lived two landings up and across, from the flat which was being used to store the 'goods' which he needed to be close to, in order to keep things running.

This was working out fine at first, and if truth be told he was really enjoying the time he spent with Carol, the sex was amazing as well, win-win for him, until he had bumped into Pete at the bar. Charlie was not for getting involved at first, when his cell mate Pete McNeil had divulged his plans when he was released, he thought this was something bigger than he had ever been involved in before, therefore it was too risky, he had no intentions of going back inside. It had taken Pete quite a while to talk him into working along -side him. Charlie eventually agreed, but only on the understanding that he was a watchman, nothing else! So, when he had saw Pete at the bar that night, he thought something was not right, as Pete never liked to be seen in the company of his employees, for risk of association. When Pete told him about the missing 'goods' he panicked. Charlie knew this was not good, that there would be repercussions from this all round, with the guys that were supposed to be watching and keeping the 'goods' safe, also with the Police, providing that they were involved now. It was not understood how this had happened, as no-one was supposed to know the goings on within the flat, so how did the 'goods' get free? That was the question Pete was wanting answered and fast! Whoever had taken their eyes off them was in big trouble, Charlie was reassuring him at the bar that it was not him! This was true, Charlie had arranged for one of the other guys to keep an eye on the flat, as he always did, whenever he was going out with Carol, so Pete made it clear it was up to him to find out what had gone wrong and more important find the 'goods'

CHAPTER EIGHT

"This is taking us into dangerous territory Vicki, I don't want you or anyone else to be placing themselves in situations they cannot get out of!" stated Dougie, as they sat all together round the desk in his office. Around him were Officer David Young, Colin and Vicki all trying to work out exactly what kind of situation they had walked into. Since Vicki had rescued the young girl Mandy, it was more important that they delved further, since it was evident that there was sex trafficking going on right under their noses. "No-one will be placing themselves in danger on purpose Dougie, but we can't ignore what we've uncovered either, how many more Mandy's are out there... right now? We have to keep going with this story...." She was aware she sounded desperate, she was. Since finding that young girl, Vicki could not think about anything else, the fear that there were more girls locked away in horrible dirty cramped flats, being forced to have sex with men, had very much became a reality and she was so enraged at this she knew there was nothing she would not do to help free them.

Mandy had divulged her story to Vicki the day she had freed her, Vicki knew she was in a better place, being taken care of properly, she had contacted Officer Young and informed him of the horrors she had uncovered on the Elton Estate. They agreed to meet at her office the next day to work out a strategy plan. Sitting here within the safe confines of her workplace, Vicki was getting more frustrated with every passing minute, at the stalemate they found themselves at. It was understandable, Dougie was going to be over protective regarding her involvement with this case now. but there was no way she was walking away from this story. If it meant she had to work alongside Colin, then she would need to suffer that, rather than be forced to give up the story all together for her own safety. The excitement was clear for all to see on Colin's face, that he was being allowed to jump on this big story, he did not mind it including babysitting Vicki, so long as his name was in print with this story, he felt he could go work anywhere, this could set him up to work for much bigger newspapers and his future would be brighter.

"Okay....as long as you and Colin work together and alongside David then we'll stay with it, BUT....and I mean this, any serious stuff gets handed over straight away to the Police....UNDERSTOOD?" Everyone looked at each other, nodding their heads replied in unison "YES! Boss". Although David was a Police Officer, he had agreed to work alongside Vicki, as long as he was the one to take it to the Serious Crime Team. Vicki was keen for this way of operating the investigation, as she realised the moment the Police were officially involved, she would not get as close to the action and this would limit her story for the newspaper.

"Where do we start?" asked Colin as they made their way from Dougie's office. "I think we need to set up some kind of surveillance on the Elton Estate, then if you... Vicki could try get access to Mandy" replied David. It was agreed that Colin and himself would take shifts at watching the Estate whilst Vicki spoke to Social Services.

Having set everything up, David would take the first shift starting that day, meanwhile Vicki was at the Social Work Department speaking to Mandy's Caseworker. It appeared she had been placed in a residential children's unit in the next town, they felt this was the best place for her, as a place of safety, they hoped that being with other children would help Mandy. Vicki would need to wait until the Social Worker had authorisation from her Senior and then ask Mandy if she wished to speak with Vicki, before she could agree to any visit from her. Not wanting to come across as pushy and spoil her chances of a meeting with Mandy, Vicki accepted this explanation and left feeling more frustrated than when she had entered the Social Work Office.

Sat in his Ford Fiesta surrounded by empty crisp and sweet wrappers, David looked around his seat and thought he was going to end up a stone heavier on this stake-out. He had been sat there in the car park of the Elton Estate, watching everyone that was going or returning for the past four hours, he was bursting for a toilet break, but he did not want to leave his post in-case he missed something relevant to this case. Unable to hold it in any longer, he found an empty Fanta bottle and relieved himself, hoping that no-one was watching him. David was just placing the now half full Fanta bottle on the passenger's side floor, when out of the corner of his eye he noticed a small stocky bald guy walking with two young girls, they looked about thirteen or fourteen years of age. It was the way in which they were walking along together, which had drawn his attention to them, and the way the girls were dressed, as they walked in unison through the car park and into the first stairwell. Both girls were scantily clothed and looked as though they were trying to look beyond their years. David thought this looked suspicious, given the age of the girls and the age of Mandy, could it just be a coincidence that they happened to be here on the same Estate looking vulnerable and scared. He decided this was worth taking a chance on, quickly leaving his car to follow in their footsteps.

The inside of the stairwell was stinking of urine, which caught in the back of his throat as he entered, the walls were covered in all kinds of graffiti and the ground had the remnants of drug paraphernalia scattered all around. David had to take care as he made his way up the staircase onto the first landing where there was no sign of them, so he fastened his pace and made it up the second stairwell onto the landing, just in time to see the bald guy push both the girls through an open door into a flat. Feeling the adrenalin pump around his body, he knew he was onto something, he had seen the horror on the faces of the girls, as they had been forced over the threshold. Casually, he walked past the door of the flat and could see the number 6 had been written on the door with a marker pen, taking a mental note of the number, he made his way back to his car to wait for Colin's arrival. and to note down all the information he had uncovered during his stint as watchman.

Meanwhile, things were not going as well for Vicki, she had been forced to return to her office and sit by the telephone, hoping that Mandy's Social Worker would contact her. Patience was never her best virtue, sitting at her desk, she could have been working, but she couldn't concentrate on anything other than the sex trafficking case. The telephone rang, she answered curtly and was surprised, it was the Social Worker phoning to inform her that she could meet with Mandy, on the basis that it was supervised by either herself, if she was available, or a worker from the children's unit if she was not. This lightened her mood and she arranged to meet with Mandy that evening.

The journey to the children's unit went by in a flash, as she thought about the questions she wanted to ask, she pondered the possibility that the Social Worker might not think them appropriate. If she worded them correctly, she thought she could get away with asking them, as it was important, she got the answers, in order, to stop the traffickers from doing further harm to other girls. The children's unit looked like all the other houses surrounding it, she assumed this was a good thing, and the kids that were placed here would not see it as different or intimidating. Walking up to the door, she couldn't help but think what the young kids must feel, as they arrived at the front door to the unit, she knew the staff tried their best to establish effective working relationships with the kids whilst trying to create a caring environment. The big red door was opened by a female care worker. She had black hair with red streaks through it, behind her stood a young boy around eight or nine years of age, peeking out at this stranger in his house. The female introduced herself as Beth and showed her the way into a small office type room, where there was a desk/chair, filing cabinet a settee and board games, it had a homely feel rather than an office one. This she later discovered was intentional, as it was important the children did not feel intimidated at all within the unit.

"Can I get you a tea or coffee Vicki? Mandy will be down in five minutes...." Vicki was digging into her bag, to get her note pad and pen, "Yeah.... that sounds lovely Beth, two sugars and milk please" finally, pulling them from her handbag, she placed them on the desk in front of her. Mandy appeared at the door looking sheepish, Vicki stood up asking her to come into the room, pointing towards the settee. As Mandy sat on the settee, Vicki walked towards her," Is it okay if I come and sit beside you Mandy, would you mind?" she felt it was vital that she gave a certain amount of control to Mandy, as she had not had any, when she was in the hands of the traffickers. "Okay" came the reply, almost a whisper, she had to strain to hear it. Taking her writing materials from the desk, Vicki moved over to the settee and sat next to Mandy, but not too close that she was invading her space.

Beth entered, placing the cups on the desk, along with a plate of biscuits. "Ohh... they biscuits look good, think I'll have one, what about you Mandy?" Vicki was trying to help Mandy feel more at ease, she got her cup of tea and offered Mandy the plate of biscuits to choose from. They sat chatting about tv programmes and films, once the tea and biscuits had been consumed, she could see Mandy was slightly more at ease, Vicki asked her to explain how she had come into contact, with the two men and if she knew their names. Mandy re-iterated the information she had told Vicki on the first day, however, now that she had time to calm down she was more forthcoming, "It was mostly Mick, he was the small fat one that was there that day, he would come and get me to take me to places or sometimes he brought men to the flat...." Vicki was writing as fast as she could, as she listened to the horrors, that Mandy had endured daily. "Do you know his second name or hear other names mentioned?" was the next question she asked, after Mandy had divulged her horror stories, she was keen to get names so that she could identify these imbeciles, with the help of David and Police information. She was certain once they found out their names, it would be a matter of time before they were caught and locked up forever. Mandy remembered the other guy there on the day, but he had always been referred to as 'Boss', no name was ever mentioned for him, however, she did recall hearing him and Mick talk about a 'Charlie', but again there was no second name. Beth had sat quietly behind the desk, writing all the information which Mandy was divulging and recording it onto her personal log, which was procedure within the care home. At this point she signalled to Vicki, it was time to stop asking questions, as she could see Mandy had been put through enough for the time being. They both praised

Mandy for being so brave and reassured her that she would never have to endure anything with those horrible animals again. After chatting and laughing at Beth for her awful taste in music, Vicki said her goodbyes, vowing to visit Mandy again soon, only if she wanted her to. Mandy was happy with this and seemed more settled as Vicki was leaving, perhaps, talking about what had happened to her had helped her a little, Vicki hoped this was the reason. On her drive home Vicki was thinking about the information she had gathered from Mandy, when she was brought back to the moment by the sound of Taylor Dayne's 'Tell It To My Heart'. Listening, she began singing and thinking about Michael, she had not seen him since the night he had taken her out for dinner and then the cinema, she made herself a promise to get in touch with him, because he was a good guy and she didn't want to let him go.

CHAPTER NINE

Normally, a Saturday morning consisted of a long lie in her bed, some love-making then they got up, dressed and would eat breakfast at a café in town. This morning was different in more ways than one. Last night Carol had made a big effort in the way she looked, Charlie had not been as attentive as he had previously, and she decided she would show him that she was worth his effort and affection. After work on the Wednesday. she had gone into Town, as a new clothes store had opened, and everyone was saying how gorgeous the clothes were inside, so Carol lifted the money that she had put away in the tin in the cupboard for her gas and electricity, knowing full well this would have repercussions for her later in the month. The thought that Charlie was losing interest in her made her anxiety heighten to the point she could hardly breathe, making her chest tighten, she had to hold onto him, she needed him! As she had dressed in her new sequinned mini dress, Carol felt a million dollars, she had spent time doing her hair and her make-up, she knew she looked good! When she had heard him chapping on the door last night, her heart was fit to burst with the excitement of him seeing her new dress and how she looked. Unfortunately, as she opened the door, Charlie hardly noticed her, let alone what she was wearing or how good she was looking. He walked straight into the living room, over towards the window, where he stood glaring out without saying a word. This infuriated her, she couldn't let him treat her like this, "Well, people usually say Hello or something as they come in through a door!" she was raging, she could feel herself shake, no reaction, he was still more concerned with looking out the window than her. "Did you not hear what I said...." She knew she was pushing him, but she had spent all of her money and time, the least he could do was acknowledge her. "What you on about now?" he replied, without looking away from the window, "Is there something more interesting out the bleeding window, than in this room?" Still he stood staring out of the window. "Charlie!" finally, he turned around, his face was far from happy looking. "I've gone to a lot of trouble trying to look good for you and you don't even give me one look, what is your problem, every time you're here you're bleeding checking out the Estate more than me!" she had started, so she may as well finish, she thought. He walked up towards her and suddenly his facial expression softened as he held out his arms, "Of course Babe, I'm sorry, I was miles away just so much in my head, you know me...." Placing his arms around her waist he pulled her in closer and kissed her on the lips. "How could I not notice you, you're gorgeous and so sexy all the time...come here" he grabbed her down into the settee and began kissing her neck, her bad mood evaporating with every kiss, she never could resist, and he knew it! They had eventually made it to the pub, then they had gone onto 'Malibu' but there were times throughout the night when Charlie's mind appeared to be somewhere else or was it someone else, she vowed she would find out.

Lying in Carol's bed staring up at the ceiling, a thousand thoughts racing through his mind, Charlie could not stop thinking about the 'goods', as Pete called them, and where the hell they had gone to and how? This was consuming his every thought, he was feeling totally frustrated at the lack of explanation he had been given from that bone-head Mick. Apparently, she wouldn't have been fit to go anywhere herself after the beating Pete had given her, and she had been locked in, that was Micks' excuse and it was no help to him. The fact that Mick was being so blaize about the missing girl, was infuriating him more, given that he felt that he was being left to clean up their mess. Now, after seeing Mick leading another two girls into the flat, as he had made his way here last night, the anger was building up inside him, he was struggling, trying to push it down and act normal, as he worked out a way of finding the girl, and ensuring no-one found out about this chaos he had found himself bang in the middle of. This was not feeling right....

Last night, just as he had parked his car and was walking up to Carol's flat, he had seen Mick, with another two young girls, heading in the direction of the 'safe house' only it appeared it wasn't that safe, so why the hell was he taking them up there? He was asking himself this question, as Carol had opened her door. Heading straight into the living room, Charlie was able to watch Mick escort them into the flat and shut the door. *Jeezo, what a feckin dumbwit*!!, he was saying to himself, all the while trying to keep his frustrations from blowing. Charlie couldn't believe the stupidity of both Mick and Pete. *What the hell have I got myself into here, with these two fuckwits?* he asked himself, all the while Carol was going on about something which he had not even heard, because he was so enraged and frustrated at what he had witnessed. It hadn't been until she had shouted his name, that he had turned to see her standing looking like she had spent a lot of time and effort on herself, but it was clear to see she was far from happy. It was then he was forced to place Mick's activities to the back of his mind, as he needed Carol and more so this flat, he had to keep her on side and he always knew how to keep her sweet.

Deciding he was going to get out of Pete's masterplan, after all he was only meant to be a minor player in this, it felt like he was being used to clean up their mistakes and being dragged further in, this was not what he signed up for! Charlie got up, dressed and left Carol's place without having anything to eat. He was working on the adrenalin rush. he was getting from working out his exit plan away from this trouble. He quickly placed a kiss on Carol's cheek and told her he would be back late, then proceeded down the stairwell heading into Town. After he had finished his business in there he intended to come back and have a word with Mick himself...

Sitting in her car on the Elton Estate, Vicki was enjoying her stint as undercover reporter. This was what she had become since Colin had work to finish for a story due this week, it was decided she would take his shift on the Estate, once she had ensured them, she would not place herself in danger. At first when she had arrived on the Estate, she enjoyed people watching, the different cultural ways in which people were dressed, the brightly coloured clothes, the small children, the way they held onto their mums' hands tightly. It seemed there were many different nationalities, all living on top of one another in such a confined space. The buildings all looked neglected, with some brickwork crumbling off the outer buildings, she wondered what the insides were like, probably covered in damp, which wouldn't make for a comfortable environment to live in. Boredom was setting in, she was too afraid to put the car radio on in-case the battery went flat, she did not wish to be stranded here alone at night. Looking over at the stairwell where David had reported the man had gone up with the two young girls, she saw a well- dressed woman walk out from it. There was something oddly familiar about the way she was walking, she could not stop herself from staring at her, as she made her way in the direction of Vicki's car the realisation hit her, she could not believe her eyes, *OH MY GOD!*... was all she repeated to herself, as she watched her old friend Carol, walk straight by her, without noticing she was in the car. *Bloody Hell! What's she doing here?* she asked herself, in shock and disbelief, at the sight of her old friend after all these years. Vicki had not seen or spoken to Carol for a few years, mainly due to Carol's inability to move forward after the Court case, and the way in which Carol had withdrawn into herself. Seeing Carol, she felt taken aback at the sight of her and sad because she felt she had missed an opportunity to speak to her again. *I wonder what she was doing here, does she live here? If she does, I'll probably see her again...*she was talking to herself, she had a lot of questions she'd like to ask Carol, should their paths ever cross again. It was getting late, and the night sky was drawing nearer, she could hardly feel her bum, it was numb from sitting so long in this confined space, her back was beginning to really hurt as well. Vicki decided she was calling it a night, but as she put her key in the ignition, just about to start the engine, she noticed a male figure walking towards the stairwell she had been focused on all night. Looking from where she was he matched the description of the male that David had seen earlier with the two girls, *Small...stocky build, bald, wearing the same kind of bomber jacket...* she ticked them off in her head, *Yip, definitely matches the description...NOW What?* the adrenalin was coursing its way through her body, as she tried hard to remain calm and think straight. Vicki decided to remain where she was, in her car, and observed the area, to go after the guy would be too dangerous alone, she had vowed to keep herself as safe as possible today, this felt right and if she saw anything untoward, she would make notes and return with David. It was getting darker, the Estate was not exactly the brightest lit place, her eyes were beginning to hurt as she strained them, in order not to miss the guy leave the building again. Time was going by, Vicki was getting anxious and worried. In the time the guy had gone up the stairs, she was wondering whether the girls were up in the flat, and if they were. what horrors were being forced upon them, whilst she was sitting here in her car. Eventually, before midnight, the guy appeared from the stairwell, she felt relieved that he was alone, but then again there had been people coming and going all evening. Relief was short lived, as anyone of them could have been visiting the flat! Vicki wrote the time and a short description of the guy in her filofax, to pass onto the team later. Watching the guy, she saw him stop in his tracks and turn, as though someone had called on him, she then saw another male come from around the corner of the car park, he walked up to the guy, from where she was sat, they looked like they knew one another. *Oh! this is interesting! Who the hell is this now?* She was asking herself, writing down, as fast as she could, the approaching guys description. He was quite good looking, from what she could see, tall, with dark hair, his clothes were fashionable and not cheap looking either, he was a league above the guy she had under surveillance, perhaps this was the leader of the gang. Both men stood talking for a few minutes, then began walking straight in the direction of her car. *Shit! Please don't notice me...* she was pleading, as she tried to slide down the driver's seat as slowly and gently as she could, the last thing she needed was for them to notice her. Lying half way down the seat, she could see just above the dashboard, the two guys were deep in discussion, but she could not make out what was being said, with the new guy doing most of the talking. *Whoa... that was close!* she heard the Irish lilt, as the new guy spoke louder. It was the Irish accent which had made her stop what she was thinking. She could see the guy clearer now, as they were by her car under a street light, *"Mother of God!! IT CAN'T BE!!"*

In her car, back aching from the position she was lying in, Vicki was in total shock! *Charlie Sweeney! How the hell has he turned up here?* It did not matter how many times she repeated this question to herself, no answer was to be found. She was so tired from sitting here watching all night, her brain was not functioning properly, she needed to go home to try get some sleep, but she knew that would be difficult now. Quickly, she wrote about what she had witnessed with the two men, adding a big question mark, as she wrote in block capitals.... CHARLIE SWEENEY?

CHAPTER TEN

The ringing of the telephone from down the hallway awoke Vicki the next morning...Lying in her bed she was struggling to feel awake as she had little sleep, due to a replay of what she had witnessed the previous night. Charlie Sweeney... she could not get the sight of him out of her mind and no matter how many times she asked herself. For the life of her, she could not understand why and what he was doing on the Elton Estate, but from her knowledge of him she knew it had to be trouble! Slowly, she got out of her bed and made her way to the persistent ringing of the telephone, "Hello", she answered, "Hi is that you Vicki? Its Michael I thought I'd give you a call since I haven't heard from you in a few days..." he sounded nervous, she thought. "Hi Michael... yeah I've just been a little busy with work stuff "she replied. "I suppose the chance of seeing you is out the window then?" he was a nice guy, but right now she had more important things going on, she knew she did not have the time to give Michael. "MMmm... Can I take a rain check and call you when I'm not so busy, I'm stuck in the middle of something really serious, this could be my big break, I need to stay focussed Michael I'm sorry" she hoped he would not take this personally, at the moment she sensed she was onto something big, she could not afford any distractions. They chatted briefly and ended the call with both saying they would keep in touch, until they could eventually meet up.

As Vicki made her way back to her bedroom, she began wondering if she had done the right thing, not going out to see Michael, then her mind went back to the previous night and she felt sure she had made the right decision. The girl's lives mattered more to her at the moment. *Somethings' can wait*! she told herself, she grabbed some clothes and went into the bathroom to get washed and ready for the day ahead. "Are you not going to have some breakfast Missy?" Vicki's Mum worried about her daughter, the way in which she seemed to be flinging herself into her work, she felt she should be going out and enjoying herself, instead of constantly working, the way she had of late. "Mum I'll get something in work, I promise, stop worrying" Vicki knew her Mum was concerned for her well- being. There was no way she could divulge any information from what she was working on, or what she had been up to! If her Mum found out she had seen Charlie Sweeney again, she would not let her out of the house, let alone go to work on the case. "I'll try be home earlier tonight" she called, as she closed the front door behind her, making her way to the office.

"Have you anything to report then?" Dougie sat behind his desk, looking perturbed, whilst Vicki remained standing at the other side. Looking at his face, she knew she had to tell him everything, or she could be taken off this story. He was anxious because of the dangerous element of the story, he did not like placing her in situations where he would not feel comfortable himself, and after she had relayed the previous nights' events, he felt even unhappier and worried about her working on the case. "Vicki, I think it's time we let someone else take this from you," he was aware of her history, and what the name Charlie Sweeney meant to her. "NO! I have worked really hard at finding these leads Dougie, it's my story, there's no way I'm just going to hand all my work over to someone else!" she was furious, struggling to keep her emotions from showing. "I've done all the leg work on this, I'm the one who has the contacts, please Dougie…. I've been safe up to now, I can handle the fact Charlie Sweeney may be involved, but we don't know for sure if he is yet", she was pleading again, her heart was racing, as she pled her case, she tried hard to convince him to allow her to remain on the story. After several long minutes, which had felt like hours to her, he finally agreed to let her stay with the story, as long as she agreed to stay safe, and that the minute it got too much for her, she admitted it and stood back. Vicki jumped at this chance, she knew deep down there was no way in hell she would back down, but she felt less convinced about keeping herself safe. In the back of her mind she knew she would need to face Charlie Sweeney one way or another, she had to find out what his involvement with those girls was, and she would!

"Carol! Carol!" he called making his way along the hall into the bedroom, checking she was not there from behind the door, *Nope not here by the looks of it, Thank God!* he smirked, walking into the living room and straight up to look out of the window. Since she had given him the spare key to her flat, life had been a lot easier, especially keeping an eye on the "goods". This was his vantage point, he could see down onto the landing where the girls were being kept, it allowed him the opportunity to keep an eye on the goings on, without having any direct contact. This suited him, as the last thing he wanted was to go back inside and he had realised the only way he could remain on the outside, was to take the kind of action which he had taken.

Better put the telly on, make it look like I'm arsing about... Switching the tv on to the sound of the "Quantum Leap" starting, he continued watching out of the window. Hearing the front door open and close, he stepped back from the window, threw himself onto the settee, lying with his feet up. "That You Babe?" she asked, "You had better hope it is or your being robbed" he replied sarcastically, making her way over to where he lay, she removed his feet from the settee and sat next to him. "What time you get here at then?" Carol took off her shoes and swung her legs round to snuggle in closer to him. "Dunno, about half an hour ago, just watching this crap, why?", "No reason just asking, give us a cuddle then" Carol wrapped her arms around him and placed her head on his chest, as he lay wondering how much longer he could go on lying to her the way he was. Both had nodded off and woke up with the sound of Police sirens. Charlie almost threw her up into the heavens, as he sprung off the settee to the window. What he saw made his heart rate soar with panic, he noticed he was sweating, as he took in the four Police cars and Officers, which were making their way towards this block of flats. Charlie felt like his throat was constricting, swallowing frantically, "Charlie! What's going on?" asked a sleepy Carol, who was still lying on the settee. When she looked up and over at him, she panicked, "Charlie! You ok? "It was quite clear he was not okay, but she did not know what else to say, as he struggled to breathe. "Here, breathe into this!" she lifted a brown paper bag from the table, emptied the apples onto the floor and gave it to him. Somewhere in her memory she remembered that breathing into a paper bag helped reduce your breathing, if it was a panic attack, she thought this might be one, and if it were not then she would need to run to call for an ambulance. "Breathe slower Charlie, this'll help, slow...slow..." trying to remain calm herself, she spoke reassuringly and led him onto the settee to sit down. After a while, his breathing was returning to normal, the colour of his face not so red, Carol wondered what had just happened and why.

Sitting breathing into the paper bag, he was listening to hear if their door was going to be knocked by the Police. The only noise he could hear was his own breathing and Carol counting to three, he wished she'd shut up, so that he could find out if they were near their place or not. Slowly, his breathing returned to normal, "Carol, that's enough counting, what's going on out there?" nodding in the direction of the window. Carol got to her feet, went to the window and looked out. "Looks like a raid of some kind downstairs..." his breathing was quickening again, he placed his mouth over the bag and began inhaling again, *This is a fucking nightmare!* he repeated over and over in his head, this was not calming him, but making him worse, he knew he had to calm down to find out what was happening, but the more he thought this, the more uptight he became.

CHAPTER ELEVEN

"Put that volume down a bit James, I'm trying to think here" came the holler from Mum, sat in her favourite chair, as they all sat watching, "Baywatch". It was the times like these, when they were all together, that she had noticed her Mum became more animated and happier, almost like old times, probably because it took Mum back to when they were all kids. Changed days nowadays, with James working on the building sites, John living away in Edinburgh at University, and her working hard to become a fully- fledged Journalist, these nights were rare and precious to every one of them, but more so for Mum. "Here Vicki, come over here and help me find this word, will ye?" asked her Mum, nodding towards her seat, waving her word puzzle book. Vicki found what her Mum had been looking for in seconds and went back to lying on the settee, between John and James sat either side on armchairs.

"Did you manage to record all the charts John?" she asked, because he was the one most into his music. He spent every Sunday evening trying to record the charts without the DJ speaking, it had become a standing joke now, as he very rarely recorded the full chart without it! "Aye very good Vicki, I had all the latest ones I like done, then the eejit DJ goes and talks before the last chorus! Why the need for chat during a record, I don't feckin know!" he was raging, "Probably so that no-one gets the song free, means you need to go buy the actual record.... if you want to hear it, without someone chatting John" James replied, through laughter, they all thought this was hilarious and always asked their Mum on a Monday, if John had beaten the DJ. "One of these days John," said Mum, trying to hide her face behind her word puzzle book. Just as the programme finished, the telephone rang in the hall. "Who's that at this time of night?" asked her Mum, to no-one in particular. John got up from his seat and went to answer it. "Vicki...it's for you ", he shouted down the hall, "There's a surprise... eh?" he remarked, as she passed him in the hallway. Sticking her tongue out at him, she lifted the receiver, "Hello," she was surprised to hear Michael Gold on the line. Mainly because of the time of night, but also because she had not called him in weeks and thought he would have moved his sights onto someone new. "Hi Vicki, I know its late, but I thought I'd phone to tell you about the drug raid on the Elton Estate tonight...", she was puzzled as to why he thought she needed to know about this. "Oh! I haven't heard anything about this until now Michael. Is there a reason why I should have?" the curiosity was getting the better of her, she was too tired to play games. "I thought that was the Estate you were busy working on with your story and this was the reason", now she was extremely perplexed, as to his reasoning for phoning, she had not told him anything about the case. "I don't believe I have told you anything about my work Michael, other than I'm working hard on a story, I'm sorry if you have felt my work has side tracked you, but I really am busy and its nothing to do with this drug raid. To be honest I'm puzzled, as to why you would call, even if it was!" now there was no holding her back, her gut was telling her to careful and not to trust this guy. "Listen Michael, it is late and I'm tired, we can discuss this another time maybe..." Eager to get off the phone, she ended the call, totally bewildered with a million questions, as to why that conversation had taken place in the first place. Returning to the living room, she tried enjoying the rest of the evening with her family, but there was something niggling away in her mind, she knew she'd get hardly any sleep again.

In the morning Vicki was still thinking about the phone-call she had received from Michael as she ate breakfast, as she got dressed and drove into work it was still there... WHY? ...Over and over again, the same question. It was strange, that he had he felt the need to call her so late in the evening with the news of the drug raid, she could not fathom out his real reason for doing so, but she intended to find out WHY!

"Any of you guys got any further information on the drug raid on the Elton Estate last night?" was her first sentence, as she walked into the office. Colin was sat at his desk, looked up," There were two arrests for possession and handling, but they never got the guy they were after, from what I've heard" he stated. "Who are they after?" was Michael the guy they were looking for, she wondered. This sounded extreme even to her, but after a sleepless night thinking about everything she knew about him, she could not say for sure he wasn't the guy. It had occurred to her during the night, as she tossed and turned, that she never really knew much about Michael Gold. Every time they had been together, she realised now that she had been the one doing most of the talking. At the time she thought this was great, a guy who was actually listening to what she had to say, she felt special, he had made her feel special. *Was this all part of his plan? Was she part of his plan? Was there EVEN a plan?* Her head was starting to hurt from too much thinking, she needed to have a lie down, but her day was only beginning.

Vicki was struggling to concentrate, which did not go unnoticed by Dougie at the team meeting. "Earth calling Vicki...Come in Vicki!" she looked up, Dougie was standing, looking at her amusingly, "Oh! so your back in the room Miss Carey! Do you have any further information on the trafficking case?" he asked. "Nothing since my last debrief Boss, I am going back to the Estate today, I intend going in on the back of the drug raid which took place last night. People might be more open to talk today", she had a few things she wanted to keep an eye on, in that Estate.

Carol quickly turned over in her bed to turn off the alarm which was bleeping loudly, she wasn't ready for today to begin, she had hardly slept, she was still worried about Charlie after last nights' sudden panic attack. Once he had calmed down, she had asked him why it had happened, however, she was not sure he had told her the whole truth of the matter. Apparently, he started having panic attacks in prison, he said the sight of the Police cars and the sound of the siren, must have caused last nights' episode, but she felt he was holding something back. Slowly, she got out of bed, shuffled out of her bedroom, through to the living room, where Charlie was sleeping on the couch fully clothed. Standing wiping sleep from her eyes, she moved towards the couch, looked down at Charlie's sleeping face, peacefully unaware of the fact he kept her awake most of the night, with worry and questions whizzing through her mind. In the back of her mind she knew he was up to no good, the way in which his behaviour had changed since the night they had met that guy in the pub. He was jumpy at the least little noise and increasingly irritable with her, she realised his outburst last night was extreme, he had been through a lot, but she wasn't buying into his story! As she stood pondering what to do next, Charlie stirred in his sleep and turned over onto his side, bringing her back into reality, one which was becoming more and more confusing, as the days went by. Carol shook her head, turned and walked into the kitchen to make some breakfast for herself, all the while thinking back to her life before Charlie, and her life now. There was no denying, she loved him because she did with all her heart, but and it was slowly becoming a big BUT, she had to ask herself, especially this morning, did she know the man she had given her heart to, she had to admit to herself she wasn't honestly sure! This and the questions whizzing through her mind scared her, she could feel her own anxieties taking hold of her again, she didn't like it one bit, but she was not sure where to go, or who to turn to....she had been here before and she had made a promise to herself, she would always walk away from becoming embroiled in someone else's problems. The fact was she loved this man, and however much she wanted to walk away from him, she knew she couldn't, her heart would not allow her!

CHAPTER TWELVE

The traffic was horrendous and moving slowly, as Vicki sat in her car, the window wipers swishing backwards and forwards, in a desperate attempt to keep the torrential downpour of rain at bay. The dull cold weather was not helping to make her feel any better, as she struggled with the lack of a decent night's sleep. She was trying hard to motivate herself and feel energised enough to get her thinking brain back on, and find out what the hell was going on, in the Estate she was headed for. Pulling into the car park at the front of the Estate, she switched off the engine and leaned backwards into the car to grab her satchel. *Right! ... You can do this...* she was telling herself, although she felt like she was kidding herself on. Her heart was not on this fact -finding job today, her mind was still trying to figure out what Michael Gold was up to, she would not rest until she found out! Part of the problem was that she really liked him, she had begun thinking of him in a more romantic manner, in the past few weeks. Vicki did not give herself easy, she had to trust a guy before things got serious and were taken to the next level, however, recently she had caught herself daydreaming of Michael and her together... what kind of lover would he be? He always made her feel special, she had to admit to herself, he did make her stomach flip, whenever she set eyes on him. Vicki knew there was potential for an intimate relationship between them, this being the reason it was tugging at her heart, not just her mind.

Running from her car, she made her way up the first stairwell, where the smell of urine was overpowering, making her eyes watery and her nostrils constrict. *How the hell does anyone put up with this and live here...* she asked herself, taking the stairs two at a time. On the first enclosed landing she began knocking on doors to no avail, either people were not in, but given that the majority of residents on the estate were unemployed or mothers with young children, she presumed they were in and refusing to answer the door. Vicki couldn't blame them either, she would not be too eager to divulge anything she had witnessed, if she had the misfortune of living here. The fear factor was evident, as she went from door to door, with not one answered. *I'll try one more landing...* she told herself, looking at her red knuckles, which were aching from the constant knocking on the doors. Racing up the next stairwell, which was smelling just as bad as the first one, she was relieved to reach the second landing which was open, allowing her the luxury of a clear lungful of fresh air.

Feeling deflated, Vicki moved slowly from door to door, with no success, just more painful knuckles. Taking a moment to stand and rub her hands, Vicki took in her bird's eye view of the Elton Estate. It was clear to see the poverty which existed within the place. There were the remnants of a kiddies play area. which was vandalised and had all kinds of rubbish lying on the ground. She could see empty alcohol bottles and cans, she could imagine the local youths hanging about here, as there was nowhere else for them to go, there was no way in heaven the area was suitable for any kids to play there, especially small kiddies. As she took in her surroundings, Vicki's attention was drawn to a female figure walking towards the stairwell to the landing she now stood. Taking a deep breathe, she straightened herself up and began walking towards the stairwell, *Play this cool and it'll pay off...fingers crossed...*she told herself, as the sound of high heels clicking made their way towards her.

Speeding up her pace. she was pretending to be rushing, as she "accidently" bumped into the female, "Oh! I'm so sorry!" exclaimed Vicki, lifting her eyes... she came face to face with Carol!

Time seemed to slow down in that precise moment, as the two women stared in disbelief at the other. "Oh My God! Carol! "Vicki exclaimed, taking in her old friend. Carol looked older, the years had not been kind to her, her clothes did her no favours. *Mutton dressed as lamb...* had been the first thought, which went through Vicki's mind, as she had watched the female figure approaching the stairwell, now she had identified that same figure as her oldest friend. Vicki wondered what kind of life Carol had been living all those years between then and now!

"Vicki! It is you...isn't it?" Carol took a step towards Vicki, screwing her eyes up inquisitively, disbelief written all over her face. "Well...Well...Well..." shaking her head from side to side, laughing softly, Vicki placed her satchel on the ground and opened her arms out, as she welcomed her friend into an embrace. Both women held onto the other and time stood still, it felt good holding Carol once more, she didn't want to let her go again. It was Carol who withdrew first, taking a step back, she stared into Vicki's eyes, "I never, ever thought I'd see you again Vicks, I wasn't sure where you were, or if you'd want to see me again, never mind come looking for me..." she stated, the disbelief and glee clear to see. Vicki was just about to correct her, but thought better of it, she could see what this chance meeting meant to Carol, she didn't have the heart to tell her the real reason why she was stood on the Estate. "I've always wondered what happened to you Carol, when I found out you were living here, I thought I'd take my chance to try find you ". She amazed herself at how easily she could lie and felt terrible guilt, but sometimes you had to be cruel to be kind and this was one of those times! Grabbing her arm, Carol guided her onto the next stairwell, up to the next landing, towards a white door with the paint peeling off. Vicki's heart was racing, she was totally unaware if Carol lived alone or with a partner. She felt awkward, given the fact she had lied and was overwhelmed seeing her old friend. The situation was far from ideal, her apprehension increased, with ever footstep towards the door. Removing her keys from her coat pocket, Carol excitedly opened the shabby door into a small narrow purple hallway, which led her into a big brighter living room. Looking around the living room, Vicki noticed how old and worn the furniture appeared, yet the couch looked comfortable and overall the flat had a homely feel to it...*shabby chic*...she thought!

"What do you think of my humble abode? It's not quite what I had in mind, when I used to think of my own home, but it's cosy, if you don't look out of the window" Carol laughed, trying to cover her embarrassment at living on the Estate. Moving over to the couch, Vicki sat looking around the room, "It's nice and homely Carol, I like it and at least you have your own place, I'm still at my Mums!" Although she often thought about moving out from her Mum's house, financially Vicki knew she couldn't afford to live on her own, and deep down she didn't feel ready to leave her Mum, she'd miss her and everything she does for her. "Do you fancy a cuppa Vicks? I've got some nice biscuits in" Vicki nodded her head in approval. Now that she was in the flat and it was just the two of them her nerves had settled, she was glad she had bumped into Carol again, it was good to see her, but she could sense Carol's anxiety, she wasn't sure if it was due to her being here in her home or if there was another reason.

The kettle was boiling, as she was getting the milk from the fridge, Carol tried to stop her hands from shaking. Walking over towards the kitchen worktop, she was shaking her head from side to side in disbelief, she was finding it hard getting over the shock that Vicki had come looking for her after all these years. They had lost touch gradually breaking away from one another all those years back, mainly due to herself, the way in which she had basically locked herself away from the world. It was for the sake of her own sanity, she told herself, she may not be here today if she had carried on pretending everything was alright. It was the right thing for her and the years of counselling and healing herself was paying off, she was in a much better place mentally. Maybe Vicki and her could start afresh, or perhaps too much water had passed under that bridge, only time would tell she thought to herself. Carol had missed her friend and had often wondered what she was doing with her life...Now she had the opportunity to rekindle the friendship, she was feeling more positive than she had at the beginning of the day. It would be good to have Vicki back, wait until she told her who her boyfriend was...she could not wait to see the surprise on Vicki's face when she dropped that bombshell.

"What do you take in your tea Vicks?" Carol called through from the kitchen. "Milk and two please..." Vicki replied. Sitting in the living room on her own. Vicki was looking for signs of a man or kids living with Carol, there was nothing to indicate either. Just as she was getting to her feet to look out of the window, Carol entered carrying a tray with two mugs and a plate of milk chocolate digestives. "Wait and I'll give you a hand..." she offered, reaching over she took the tray from Carol's shaking hands, whilst Carol pulled a small table over. "So how long have you been living here then?" "Ohhh... must be coming up for five years now...I moved out just after Tracey, it was needed Vicki, in order to try help myself, you know..." Vicki knew what she meant, Carol had to gain confidence and moving out to live here on her own was a brave thing to have done. She sensed Carol had been through a tough time and hoped she was in a better place...mentally. So far from what she had seen, it looked as though her old friend was winning the fight!

"Where is Tracey now? The last I heard she had a couple of kids..." she had also heard her Husband had done a runner with her friend or neighbour, but she did not feel comfortable saying this to Carol. "Yeah she has two boys Timmy and Tommy, they're great boys Vicki, unfortunately their Dad's an arse, he ran off with her mate...it was hard, probably still is for her, not that she'll let on..." "Jeezo Carol, what a fecker...yeah, Tracey always tried to put on a brave face for everyone, but you could always tell when she wasn't really coping as well as she liked to make out! I hope things work out for her..." Vicki had a soft spot for Carol's big Sister, she had always tried to look out for them, when they were younger, and was a tower of strength to them when all the Jonjo stuff was going on. Vicki never could understand how a man could walk out on his Wife and kids without a backwards glance, her Dad had done the same thing, maybe this had something to do with her distrust of men, although she knew that not all men were the same, and it was his loss at the end of the day!

Hours passed before they both realised. Catching up on the years they had missed and finding out what their families were doing now, felt like old times as they sat chatting, laughing and at times almost crying, as they rediscovered their friendship. However, they each held back one piece of information...Vicki never divulged her real reason for being on the Estate that day...and Carol never told her friend the identity of her boyfriend. As Carol waved Vicki off from her front door, she wondered, how she would break the news that Charlie Sweeney was not history!

CHAPTER THIRTEEN

"I'm telling you Pete! This is getting way more dangerous than you first told me...I mean... I've not got any intentions of going back to jail for anyone man!" Charlie lifted his pint and took a large gulp, before placing it back on the table between Pete and himself. They had chosen this pub as it was out of their area, and thought they would be able to talk, without being interrupted, but they hadn't realised it was the pub's karaoke night, therefore, the opportunity for a quiet debrief was out of the question. The raid on the estate during that week had really shaken Charlie up, when he awoke to the sound of the Police sirens and saw all the coppers running around the place, he believed that he was their intended target. He was embarrassed at the way in which he had basically broke into a sheer panic in front of Carol, he thought he was in control of his mind, but the events of that night proved otherwise. Carol had been a good support, he was glad in a way, she had been there to talk him down from his anxiety and help bring his breathing and panic attack under control again. Seeing the Police and all the commotion they had brought with them, had really unnerved him, and made him realise that he wanted out of this plan of Pete's. When they had shared their cell, Pete had asked him to help with his plan, there had been no mention of girls being brought into the country, to be used for selling sex to punters. His understanding was that due to him spending so much of his jail term in the gym, the shape he was in now, he would be the "heavy" every now and again, when Pete needed the frighteners put on someone. At the time Charlie had been naïve, thinking this was some kind of drug dealing, or money laundering system that Pete was setting up, there had been no mention of human trafficking, and that was exactly what he had become drawn into. The severity of what he was now involved in, had hit him straight in the face, he knew he had to find a way out one way or another. "I hear you! big yin, it put the fear up me as well, all that carry on but there's no need to panic about it, it's all in hand... in fact there's another four wee beauty's being brought over to our patch later in the week...." Slapping Charlie's shoulder, he finished his pint and went to the bar to place another order for them both.

Feck sake...what the hell am I gonna do now? Panicking, Charlie was hoping his exterior was looking nothing like his insides felt, because inside he was frantic with fear. Taking another gulp of his pint, he tried to act as calm as he possibly could, given the circumstances, as he watched Pete turn from the bar with two more drinks in is hands. "Right! Here get that down your neck... And I'll tell you what I want you to do next..."

Driving back towards Hollowburn, Charlie's mind was racing with thoughts of how he could get out of working for Pete. During their meeting Pete had informed him of the next batch of girls which were due and his plans for them. Charlie had listened and was sickened when he heard Pete explain so matter of fact, what he expected from these girls. They were all underage with an average age of 12 years old, the fact they were being forced to perform sexually for men of all ages, made Charlie sick to his stomach. He felt sorry for them, he struggled to understand what kind of family would allow their daughters to be exported, to be used and abused like pieces of meat. This was exactly what was happening to the girls! Pete had told him that the majority of the girl's families lived in poverty, in a town within Romania, and had borrowed money from wealthy men, who then asked for their daughters in exchange for writing off their debts. The girls were told they would be brought to the UK to work to help their families, however, they were told it was cleaning and looking after children for wealthy people. Once they crossed the Border into the UK their passports were removed from their possession and kept by Bosses here, until the debt was cleared, but Charlie knew from experience that the debt was never written off, and the girls usually ended up being found beaten and dead. This was the reason why he had to find a way out, drugs were another thing entirely, this was something way more sinister and dangerous for everyone involved!

Pete had provided him with enough details that would allow him to try for a deal, if he decided to go to the coppers, but his life would not be worth living if he decided to grass... They would get to him and kill him, even if he got locked up, there were people in jail who would finish him off for grassing. *Nah...* he said to himself, as he drove into the carpark at the front of the estate, *There has to be another way...* getting out if the car and walking over towards Carol's flat, he was trying to reassure himself, he needed to sit and think which way he wanted to go.

PC Young hated being on the twilight shift. Even worse was being on the twilight shift and having to patrol an area, especially one like the Elton Estate. Tonight, he was on duty with a Community Officer by the name of Edwin Marshall, although he Community Officers had training it was not as in depth as the training a full time Police Officer experienced, this fact always made PC David Young that little bit more nervous. Walking around as night fell on the estate was not a pleasant experience for anyone, there was danger lurking around everywhere, and having a CO with him was not helping. The sounds of youths shouting and name calling each other could be heard as he turned the corner at the side of the first stairwell. Sitting on the stairs sat a group of mixed-race youths, smoking and generally being a nuisance to anyone that tried to pass them on the stairwell. "Alright, what you lot doing here tonight then?" he tried to sound calm yet in control. When faced with this many young people from the Estate, he never felt totally calm, as it was common knowledge, they often carried knives and guns, which they were not scared to use on anyone. "WE ain't causing no harm man!" shouted one of the youths, who had been sitting, on replying to him he got to his feet, an attempt to intimidate him. "Have you guys not got anywhere else to be?" he knew this could rile them depending on their mood, however, his job was to promote a safe environment for everyone that lived on the Estate or had to pass through this stairwell. "Nah, not really, have we Bros?" It was the same youth mouthing off, he presumed he was the gang leader. "Well you're blocking the stairs here and folks can't pass, so do you think you could go sit somewhere else?" as he said this he walked towards the group, they split where they sat, creating a small pathway, that he walked through to the next level of the stairwell. Community Officer Marshall followed in his footsteps, although he looked confident with his long strides, David Young knew he was far from it underneath, as was he, but they had made their point and were still in one piece. Footsteps were coming in their direction, the group suddenly all stood up and made to exit the stairwell, CO Marshall raised his eye brows and looked across at him, as though he was expecting him to know what was going on, David had no idea, but from the reaction of the group he decided they should stay where they were and see for themselves who was up ahead. "Alright Mucker...what's the story...my man?" came a loud Irish accent from the direction where the youths had all dispersed to. "Hey Charlie!" replied the ringleader, "Nothing much doing mate..., just chilling with my boys... ain't we?" he turned to take in the gang, but there was no verbal reply, just the shaking of some heads. PC Young and his CO remained on the stairwell, listening intently for further information, only to be disappointed, as the conversation did not include any new intelligence regards the reason, they were patrolling the Estate in the first place. PC Young was just about to signal for his CO to follow him away from the stairwell, when they heard the footsteps continue in their direction. Both Officers looked across at one another, then straight ahead, with the understanding they would stand their ground. Coming towards them was a tall guy with dark hair, smartly dressed and a swagger in the way in which he walked, "Evening Officers" Irish lilt to the voice, *so this is the man they had heard the ringleader call Charlie*, thought PC Young, as he nodded, he watched him swagger along the landing and into the fourth door along. "Wonder who he is?" asked CO Marshall, all the while keeping his eyes firmly on the door, where Charlie had just entered, "He's obviously somebody, given the reaction of the gang...You're thinking the same?" PC Young shook his head in agreeance, he did not know who had just passed him by, but he intended to find out!

Upon entering the flat the fresh, fruity smell of Carol's favourite bubble bath hit his nostrils, before he heard her singing away to herself, as she lay in the bath. "Well someone must've had a good day" he remarked, opening the bathroom door further, he entered and sat down upon the toilet seat, taking in the view of her lying back, her eyes closed in the bath surrounded with white fluffy bubbles, she looked happy and relaxed, he felt jealous! "Dear God!" exclaimed Carol, opening her eyes and throwing some bubbles in his direction, "You gave me a fright, sneaking in like creeping JESUS!" Charlie gave out a little laugh at her remark, which annoyed her even more. "Uch! don't be like that Honey, I thought you'd be glad to see me, I mean have you not missed me?" he moved over and gently kissed her forehead, before standing and walking into the kitchen to put the kettle on. "You fancy a cuppa?" he called through, trying to ignore the unsettling feeling he had. Seeing the coppers on the landing really unnerved him, he hoped they had not picked up on his fear, as he had passed them, time was running out for him he knew deep down he was going to have to choose a side and stick to it, sooner rather than later, he just wasn't sure which one yet!

"Oh! Wait until I tell you who joined me for a cuppa earlier...You'll NEVER guess..." replied Carol, getting out of the bath tub, she placed a towel around her and skipped into the living room. "Who? Surprise me..." he was concentrating on pouring the hot water from the kettle into their favourite mugs, leaning into the kitchen Carol teased, "OHHHH this will surprise you... Vicki Carey!" "Bloody hell Babes, that is a blast from the past, does she know about you and me?" he asked, after Carol had told him how she had literally bumped into Vicki on the stairs and had spent the afternoon catching up. "No...I didn't mention Us, to tell you the truth... we were so busy filling each other in on what we had been doing since we had last spoke and what our families were doing" she felt slightly guilty for not mentioning him to Vicki, but from the way Vicki spoke about the past events and her face when she mentioned his name, she didn't want to spoil their reunion, rightly or wrongly! "You going to be seeing her again then?" he asked, dipping his biscuit into his mug of hot tea, focussing hard getting the biscuit from the mug to his mouth, before it fell in. Carol watched in anticipation of the tea winning, because the biscuit always ended up at the bottom of the mug, she laughed to herself as she saw Charlie's face when it happened again. "Yeah, probably we swapped phone numbers, she knows where I live now...You don't have a problem with that...do you?" If he said that he had an issue with them remaining in contact, then that was his problem, she thought because she was not going to lose her friend again, if she could help it! The news that Vicki Carey was back on the scene again should not have bothered him, so why did he have a feeling of impending trouble.

Chapter Fourteen

"Vicki...the phone for you!" called her Mum from the hall, she hadn't heard the phone ringing she was miles away, thinking about Carol, Michael Gold and the hours she had lost on the case, due to her meeting Carol again, her brain was ready to combust. Lifting the receiver to her ear, she was taken aback, for the second time that day...

"Hi Vicki...thought I'd give you a call find out if you're free tomorrow to grab a coffee" his voice, she thought, this was the first time he had not sounded so self-assured. " Hi Michael, I'm busy all day tomorrow, I have a lot of work to catch up on I'm afraid..." she let her excuse hang in the air for a moment, "Ahh that's okay I just thought it would be nice to see you again, as it's been a while", Vicki felt a little guilty turning him down, but her gut instinct was screaming at her not to trust him, she had no idea why, yet she was certain she would find out soon enough. Ending her phone call with Michael, she returned to her bedroom to try sort her thoughts out, her mind was racing, she could feel the beginnings of a headache. *Bloody Michael Gold, I know you're up to something and I wish you weren't*, her feelings for him had been growing, slowly, but growing all the same. Now though she wasn't sure how she felt about him, she could feel her inner barriers rising faster than they had fallen. This saddened and frustrated her. Grabbing her pyjamas, she changed into them, pulled back her covers and fell into bed...a good night's sleep was what she needed!

Placing the receiver back onto the telephone sat on his desk, Michael felt frustrated with the lack of interest from Vicki Carey. Usually getting what he wanted came a lot easier and faster than this! Sitting back in his chair, running his fingers through his blonde hair, he was not sure how he was going to get Vicki's attention, without giving too much away. He sensed that she was onto him, he could kick himself for asking her about the raid on the Elton Estate. If she found out the truth about him and his dealings, he knew she would want nothing more to do with him.

When he had first saw her again there had been an instant attraction, he was sure of that, but she seemed to be more interested in her work than spending time with him recently, and this did not make him happy. Sure, he had work to take care of too, he understood the pressures of working to deadlines and ensuring every aspect was covered, but he also made sure he made time for play. Perhaps he found this easier, as he delegated more and had a team around him, so to speak! Getting up from his seat he left his office, entered his living room and slumped onto the big comfortable settee. As he lay there his mind was still on Vicki and how he was going to manage her, when his telephone started ringing in his office. Running through he answered the call, and quickly wished he hadn't!

Pete had received a call from Mick informing him that the coppers had been sniffing about the Estate, he knew he had to be extra vigilant after the last girl vanished, they had still not found her! This and the fact that they were due another delivery of girls in a matter of days were giving him sleepless nights. He had instructed Mick to remain in the flat and continue to keep an eye on the situation, ensuring that the girl they had in the flat, remained in the flat! Easy...NOT QUITE!

Mick decided to sample some of the gear he was meant to be selling. This he felt was the least he was due, as he had been locked up in this filthy smelly flat, with no-one for company, except the miserable little bitch in the next room, *Well I'll soon give her something to moan about,* he laughed to himself, as he set up lines of cocaine on the kitchen worktop. Each sniff he inhaled, the higher he felt, until his sexual urges kicked in. Mick loved the feeling, taking the drug gave him and it always heightened his sexual desires, to the point where nothing else mattered. Tonight, was no different in fact, he thought, it's even better, because he had what he needed right here, and no-one could stop him. Entering the room, he could see the girl was asleep on the bare mattress on the floor. She was using an old curtain from the window as a cover to try and keep warm, as there was no heating in the flat. As he approached where she lay his erection was full, he could feel its tightness against his jeans. This made him more excited, "HEY!... Wake up!... HEY!" he kicked the mattress hard, which startled the young girl awake. "Uncle Mick has come to see you and make you his special girl tonight..." as he knelt down on the mattress in front of her, the girl was terrified and began to shake with fear, as she watched him struggle to remove his denims, his bulging erection escaping from within, the last thing she remembers was screaming before he silenced her.

Pete raced up the stairwell and along to the flat. He had been trying to get a hold of Mick since they had last spoke earlier in the evening, to no avail. Concerned, he had got in his car and driven here to find out what the hell was going on. As he had pulled up into the car park, he looked around to see whether the coppers were here, happy that the coast was clear, he had made the decision to take the chance to surprise Mick. *If Mohammed won't come to the mountain...I'll bleeding well come to him...and you better not have fucked this up!*

Several knocks and still no answer of the flats' door! Pete was running on adrenalin now and panic, the sweat was beginning to run down the sides of his face.

Keep it calm man! he repeated to himself over and over, trying to slow his breathing down, he needed to calm down, so that he could think about his next move. One more knock and still no reply, not wanting to cause a scene, he found himself with no other choice, but to burst the lock on the door. Stepping back, he lunged forward with his right leg at the precise location of the lock, and burst the door open...Entering the hallway, the smell of stale food and damp were the first things to knock his senses, then the smell of urine hit him, it was pungent. He continued, further up the hallway, using the collar of his coat to protect his nostrils from the smells, it was making him feel queasy. *Christ sake what kind of hell hole was Mick keeping these girls in, surely the punters must notice the state of the place...*he asked himself, taking in the threadbare carpet and the wallpaper, which was hanging off the walls in most places. *This place was a shithole,* no *wonder the girl had made a run for it, wherever she was now had to be a step up from this place*, he decided. As he entered the kitchen, he was not shocked to find it filthy, with plates of leftover food lying about, what he presumed were worktops, as he could not actually see the surface for rubbish. He did notice however, the residue left over from the lines of cocaine and his temper began to rise. "Mick...Where the hell are you?" turning he left the kitchen angrily, marching from door to door, until he opened the last one....the sight in front of him made his stomach turn, he ran fast towards the bathroom, making it to the toilet, just in the nick of time, as he threw up! Uncertain what to do once he had composed himself, Pete left the flat, he was grateful for the opportunity to get some fresh air into his lungs. Walking to the phone box at the corner of the Estate, he knew he was left with no other option, but to inform the Gaffer, of what he had found. Pete realised this was going to make him look bad, the Gaffer would not like this one bit, but even he was shocked at the sight in the flat and it was Mick's doing, so he would ensure it was Mick who took the fall.

Having informed the Gaffer of the conditions within the flat, and the state in which he had found Mick with the girl, he wasn't surprised to hear the Gaffer explode with rage! He ordered Pete to deal with Mick for the moment, but firstly he had to get the place cleared up, and by this he meant get rid of any evidence, meaning the girl's body! Replacing the receiver and leaving the phone box, Pete was still shaking from the scene he had witnessed in the flat. Having heard every one of the Gaffers threats of what was coming to Mick for messing this up, he had to admit to himself, he was scared, not only for Mick, but for himself! He knew he had to try his best for damage limitation, this began with carrying out a decent clean up, he knew the perfect person that owed him, and would be easily motivated into giving him a hand....

Chapter Fifteen

"Charlie, was that the door? Charlie...." nudging him in his ribs, Carol was not sure if she had heard the noise or if she had been dreaming, as she had been in a good deep sleep for once. BANG! BANG! BANG! *That was definitely the bleeding door, there had better be a bloody fire for getting me out my bed*! thought Charlie as he slowly and sleepily made his way towards the door. BANG! BANG! "I'm coming! Hold your horses!" he called, undoing the locks, opening the door, he was faced with a pale faced and frightened Pete, this was the last thing he expected or needed! "Who is it at this time of the night Charlie?" called Carol from the bedroom. "It's okay Babe, just one of my mates a bit worse for wear, he'll be fine once he sleeps it off" he called back down the hall, as he ushered Pete into the living room, closing the door firmly shut behind them. "What the hell you doing here at this time? Could you not have waited at least until the morning for fucks sake Pete..." he could tell by the state Pete was in that this was serious, he had never before seen him as rattled, as he was in front of him now. This made him fear the answer to his question!

"You got anything to drink? I don't mean tea or coffee, something hard..." Pete sat himself onto the edge of the settee, ran his fingers through his hair, before looking directly up at Charlie's face, bewilderment written all over it. "Wait and I'll see what's in the cupboard, Carol's old man was an alcoholic, so she doesn't tend to keep any drink in the place", he was aware he was chattering nonsense, Pete had no interest in Carol's Dad's drinking habits, he knew it was because he was nervous, quickly he went into the kitchen and was surprised to find the remnants of a half bottle of vodka at the back of the cupboard. Looking up he saw on the kitchen clock it was coming up for 4 in the morning, thinking this was going to be a long night he poured himself some vodka along with one for Pete. Sitting across from Pete he watched and listened in disbelief at what Pete was saying. "So, I had to kick the door in. You want to see the mess of the place and the smell...Christ sake man...it's bad!" "It's always been a shithole, that's not news Pete, the punters aren't there to look at the décor are they? As long as they get a good seeing to, they're not caring if it's the Ritz or the Elton..." Charlie smirked, he couldn't understand why the state of the flat was such a surprise to Pete and why it brought him to his door in the middle of the night. "That's not the fuckin problem, you arse, once I got over the shock of the dump, I could tell that fucker Mick had been using the gear for his own personal use, he wasn't answering me when I was shouting out his name, so I had to go through the place looking for the bastard...." Pete put his head down and was shaking, Charlie thought this was due to rage, due to catching Mick red handed using the gear. Anyone within the network, from the Gaffer, who made the rules, to the young boys on the Estate they used as drug runners, understood that the gear was there for financial gains and under no circumstances to be used for personal consumption. This was always made clear at the beginning of any initiation and those involved knew the punishment for using instead of selling was never going to end well for them! "He knows the score mate, if you had to make a point of him, then he was well aware of this just the same as the rest of us, don't feel bad for whatever you've done, it's the business, right?" Charlie wanted this to be over, so that he could get back to his bed, he was knackered, and this was the last thing he needed, he was no good at consoling, he was losing precious sleep here, he just wanted Pete to get over whatever he was on and leave his flat. "It's NOT the gear! " shaking his head from side to side, Pete stared straight ahead, "He's gone mad, he's done the girl in...You need to see what the fucker's done to her Chaz, seriously, there's blood all over the room and the smell..." he ran through to the toilet and emptied the remaining contents of his stomach again. *Feckin hell!* Charlie fell back against the chair where he sat, rubbed his hands up and down his face in disbelief, at what he had heard and the situation he now found himself in.

Walking along the landing, both men were trying to get their heads around the job in hand. Pete had returned from the bathroom once he had freshened himself up, told him the rest of the horrors contained within the flat across the Estate. Hoping he was still asleep, and this was a nightmare was no longer an option for Charlie. As the fresh cold night air blew around him, he shivered and pulled his coat closer for comfort rather than warmth. Up ahead he could see the burst lock on the door to the flat as they approached it, he took a deep breath, he watched Pete do the same in front of him. Once inside Pete led him to the room in question. The sun was rising and brought some light into the room. Charlie gulped down the bile which had risen into his mouth, at the smell and the sight before him. Lying on the bed was the naked body of the teenage girl, bruised and battered, there was dried blood on her face and on her legs, which looked as though it had come from between her legs." YOU DIRTY BASTARD!" he screamed at the naked Mick, as he kicked him in the stomach. This awoke Mick with a startle, "What the fuck! ", Mick found the two men standing above where he lay on the floor at the side of the bed, where the youngsters body lay. As he tried to get to his feet Charlie's foot met with his gut once more, gasping in pain he clutched at his stomach and curled over. Charlie repeatedly kicked him whilst Mick remained curled up in a ball trying to protect himself against the blows. "Whoa that's enough for now! Let's get this place cleaned up then we can deal with this piece of shit" stated Pete, pointing at the walls, which were sprayed with the girl's blood, and then looking down to where she lay. "YOU made the problem, you should be the one to clean it up! The Gaffer's well aware of your wee spree here... I wouldn't want to be you!" Charlie wanted to put the fear into Mick, but he wasn't convinced his threat had sunk in, as Mick still looked well under the influence, he must've consumed some amount of gear last night he thought to himself.

Leaving Mick where he lay, they knew he was in no fit state to try and make an escape from them. They went in to the kitchen and after a rummage around the cupboards they discovered some bleach and cleaning fluids. Grabbing some old clothes from the drawers, they proceeded to clean the worse of the blood from the bedroom. Pete left the flat to get some black bags from the boot of his car, Charlie took this chance to confront Mick again. Entering the room, he was still lying curled up on the floor, "What did you do to that poor kid? Why? ", no reply came, "Answer me...you piece of shit! What the hell happened in here last night?" he asked again, giving him another kick, this time to his head. Mick grunted as he turned to look at Charlie towering above him, he knew there was no way out of this, he would need to comply or face the consequences, either way he was done. "I was bored... needed a bit of fun" he smirked, and felt another blow to his gut, as Charlie's foot made contact once more. "FUN! You think this was FUN for her? "More blows to his body, until eventually, Pete returned and pulled the raging Charlie off him. "C'mon Man, we've got too much to do we'll get him...don't worry, but in time, come on this first..." nodding in the direction of the girl's lifeless body. Both men struggled with their emotions, as they covered the body with the old curtain and placed it into a black bag, so small was her frame that she fitted easily inside. Pete checked outside the flat, seeing that the landing was clear, as most residents were still asleep, he signalled for Charlie to carry the bag down to his car where he placed her gently in the boot. Charlie felt relief, but he understood it was going to be short lived, unless he got out from Pete's hold. Tonight, had made his mind up for him, there was no way he was going back inside for any part of tonight, he knew what he had to do!

Chapter Sixteen

"Mum, can I borrow some money just until the end of the week?" she hated asking her Mum for cash, she liked to think of herself as Miss Independent, but she needed to find out what it was her gut was screaming at her for regards Michael. Deep down she felt something was not ringing true with her new beau, she told herself it was better she found out now, rather than later, preventing herself from being hurt by another man. "Sure Honey, I think there's enough in my purse, help yourself" Mum replied, from the kitchen, "I'm making your favourite dinner tonight, what time will you be back?" Vicki loved her Mum's Spaghetti Bolognese, but on this occasion, she would eat it for lunch tomorrow, rather than later that evening, as she had other plans for tonight. "Uch... Mum I'm going to be back late tonight I'm eating out, but save me some, I'll have it for lunch tomorrow...that okay?" she felt terrible letting her Mum down, after she was going to the trouble of cooking her dinner, but she was sure James would be calling in later, he would soon help empty the pot, as well as keep Mum company. Mum was standing at the cooker, preparing the meal, as she approached her from behind and gave her a big hug, "What's that for Missy? No need to feel bad I'll put some aside for you, before your Brother eats it all, don't worry" she gave a little chuckle, continuing to stir the pot, "Thanks Mum, I got the money, I'll try not be too late" she gave her Mum another hug before running out the front door.

In the office Vicki sat at her desk with the telephone receiver in one hand, readying herself for what she was going to say to Michael, she hoped he would accept her offer to meet up later for something to eat, she was aware she had been playing it cool ,she hoped she hadn't put him off all together. The phone was answered on the second ring," Hi Michael, it's Vicki I was hoping we could go grab something to eat later, if you're free, that is?" she was nervously wrapping the cord of the phone around her fingers, "Mmm..can I get back to you on that Vicki, I'm up to my ears in it at the moment..." he replied, she was taken aback at this rebuff,

What the hells he playing at, she asked herself, this had thrown her off, due to the fact he was always chasing her, asking her out, she was not expecting this reply one bit, neither did she like it! "Sure, no problem, I was at a loose end tonight, but we can always meet up another night, no big deal ..." *Why did I say no big deal...now he's gonna think it is...Oh my God!* She had been totally not prepared for this, and was not sure where to go from here, "I'll call you later in the week, okay?", he said, before the line went dead. *Well that was strange, did Michael did give ME a knock back*, Vicki sat bewildered, not sure what to make of this. He had been practically annoying her for weeks to meet up, now he wasn't up for seeing her, something was not right about this and she was going to find out what!

Answering the phone, Michael had been surprised to hear Vicki's voice on the other end, he was expecting an update from Pete, in regards the situation on the estate. He was knackered, as he hadn't got much shut eye last night. He was pacing up and down the floor in his office, he had four new girls being delivered later in the day, he had to make sure Pete had done his job, by cleaning up the flat and getting rid of any evidence, before the new goods arrived. If this got messed up in any way, he would be in the shit from his contacts in Romania. He could not afford for anything else to go wrong. He did not have the headspace for Vicki, at the moment, she could wait, he had bigger problems he had to deal with first. Watching the clock, as he walked the floor, his temper was increasing, he was losing his cool, patience was never his strong point, he hated waiting on others. This was valuable time being wasted, he knew there was only one thing for it, he would need to go to the flat himself, to find out what the hell was happening!

"Boss, I'm going to pay the Elton Estate another visit just now..." Vicki called into Dougie Thompson, lifting her satchel and Filofax, she didn't bother waiting for him to reply, as she thought he would try to force her to take Colin for support. Running out the door, the last thing she heard was her Editor telling her to hold up! *No way...*she laughed, feeling she had a lucky escape. The last time she was on the Estate, she had met Carol, which had resulted in her missing out on valuable snooping time. It had been great, meeting up with her old friend again, but the downside was that she was behind with her story and needed to find some new material, as her deadline was sneaking up on her. The sun was shining. as she got out of her car, she pulled her sunglasses down and walked over towards the second stairwell. *Even the sunshine cannot improve this dump...* turning her head, taking in her surroundings, she still couldn't believe Carol was living here. Never would she have imagined her friend living on this Estate, the last place she would have looked for her if she had been given the chance. The smell of urine burned her nostrils, as it always did, the warm welcome of the Elton Estate, wriggling her nose she took a deep breathe, trying hard not to exhale until she reached the safety of the open landing off the next flight of stairs. Assessing the landing, she checked to see if there were any obvious signs, helping her choose whether to begin her enquiries, left or right!

Choosing to start knocking on the doors of those on her left, had not been the start she was hoping for, as no-one was answering their doors, and she had tried four already. Aching knuckles and beginning to feel rejected, she turned around to take in the view from where she stood. The Estate was still very much asleep, the windows which did have curtains, which were few and far between, were still closed over. There was an eerie silence, which slightly unnerved her. Looking across from where she stood, she could see Carol's flat and noticed her curtains were still drawn. Just as she was about to turn and resume her door knocking, the door to Carol's flat opened, *WHAT THE HELL!!!* Leaving the flat, she could not believe her eyes, was Charlie Sweeney! *WHAT THE HELL IS SHE PLAYING AT? Charlie FLAMING Sweeney....AND she hadn't even let on...* Vicki had a hundred and one questions whizzing through her mind as she watched Charlie swagger along the opposite landing, he did not seem aware of anyone other than himself, *Typical feckin Charlie Sweeney...*she thought, *Only out for himself, he's up to something...and I won't stop until I find out what Charlie Boy!*

Turning, she hurriedly made her way back along the landing, towards the smelly stairwell, *deep breathe again...*she told herself, taking in a lung full of fresh air, she ventured down the stairs and out to the front of the estate. No sign of him! *Where's he gone?* Frantically looking around her surroundings she could not see where Charlie had gone. *DAMN!! I've bleeding well lost him!* Frustration building up within her, *I cannot believe it! Where the hell had he gone?* Shaking her head in frustration, she was raging with herself for losing sight of him, *I might have lost you for the time being, BUT I know exactly where I'll find you again*, as she headed towards Carol's flat.

CHAPTER SEVENTEEN

*Hopefully it'll be quiet and no-one will recognise me...*thought PC David Young walking on to the Elton Estate. He was well aware he was taking a chance, coming here in his plain clothes, rather than uniform, but he did not want to bring unwanted attention his way, he had only one intention today and that was to find out the true identity of the male he had encountered on his last visit to the Estate. Since that night, there was something bugging him, which he could not shake off. Unsure, as to whether it was the man's obvious influence over the gang of youths in the area or his gut instinct, which was telling him they had met before, he had yet to find out. There was definitely an air of danger about him!

First thing he noticed was the swagger....

YES! That's him! I'm sure of it. He could feel his heart racing at the first sighting of his target. He watched as the male made his way in the opposite direction from where he stood. David turned quickly on his heel and followed behind, being careful not to be noticed. The day was getting brighter and more people were out, and about which made it easier for him to mix in with and hide amongst. *This is perfect. just as I thought this was going to be like finding a needle in a haystack, you show yourself...*smirking to himself, he was careful to keep his eyes on the man, following him, as he left the Estate in the direction of the park. *What's he playing at? Nice day for a walk in the park, but,* thought David, confused as to the why the male would come to the park this early. As he entered, David saw his target approach a park bench and sit down, hands in his pockets, crossing his legs and staring into space....*Looks like a man with a lot on his mind...*David thought to himself, stopping behind a large tree to observe from a safe distance.

Checking his watch, he realised he had been sat on the bench for over an hour, with no answers coming to him. *Right fucking mess I'm in now!* was the only thing going around Charlie's mind, sitting, taking in the peace and quiet of the park, he thought this was the best place to come and sort out his head. The answers would come fast and clear with no-one around to bother his thinking process, however, it was not working out like that. Since the night he had helped Pete dispose of the young girls' body and clean up the flat he had not been able to sleep, Carol was on to him, she knew something was bothering him, she'd have a fit if she ever found out exactly what it was! Ever since the incident which had ended up with him inside the last time, Carol was never the same person, he knew this and realised if she found out about his involvement with Pete, it could send her round the bend again, not to mention she'd finish with him, which he didn't want as she had begun to grow on him, which he was surprised about, as she was only ever meant to be a means to an end. *What the hell am I going to do?* Sitting forward, he ran his fingers through his hair, feeling lost and totally confused.

What's he doing? David was asking himself, as he watched quizzically from beneath the tree. His legs and feet were sore from standing on the same spot for so long. *I'm going to have to do something, I can't stand here all day...*beginning to jog on the spot, trying to get some feeling back into his legs, he decided from what he had seen the guy obviously had stuff on his mind, he would use to his advantage " Hi...anyone sitting here?" signalling with his hand towards the bench, right next to the guy. "No Mate, help yourself..." replied Charlie, mind still puzzling through his options, not taking any real notice of the man sitting down next to him. "Quiet here today..." David spoke, trying to open a conversation, "It is that..." replied Charlie, *Fuck off! I don't want a fucking pal...*this was the last thing Charlie needed right now, someone who wanted a chat. *Wait...*thought David, turning taking a closer look he was certain he knew him from before. David, having had a good look at the man and upon hearing the Irish accent, realised his identity, and was certain that he and *Charlie Sweeney* would be crossing paths again soon.

CHAPTER EIGHTEEN

Opening the door, Carol was surprised to find Vicki standing there. They had said they would keep in touch, *someone's keen*, she thought inviting her friend inside. "This is a lovely surprise, fancy a cuppa?" she asked, as they walked towards the living room. "Yeah cuppa would be good, then I think we need a chat...." *OHH I don't like the sound of this...*thought Carol, going into the kitchen. Coming back through carrying the tea tray, Carol could see from Vicki's demeanour that something was bothering her. Vicki was sitting upright on the edge of the settee, with a stern face, Carol was beginning to wish she hadn't answered the door. *Right let's get this over with...*thought Carol placing the tray on the coffee table between them. "Help yourself to what you need", she said wishing for this visit to end. Vicki could tell Carol was nervous, making her more curious as to what she was trying to hide from her. "So... here's the thing Carol...I'm working on something which brought me to the estate this morning, I was up in the block opposite here and happened to look over at your place, imagine my surprise..." she stopped, as Carol sat across from her, nodding her head, "Do you know what I'm going to say?" glaring over at her, " No..." replied Carol, rather sheepishly. "I think you do, Carol enough lies! You know I saw Charlie Sweeney leaving here this morning...Why was HE here?" blank look, from Carol, " What are you doing...letting him stay?" she was struggling to keep her composure, she hated liars, and felt that Carol had lied to her face when they had spoken about him, the last time she had sat here. "I was going to tell you Vick, honestly I was, but I could see how mad you were when his name was mentioned, I didn't know how to say..." swallowing and taking a deep breathe, Carol sat, head bowed, and continued, "I've been seeing Charlie for a while now, he came into my work and we just clicked..." she was scared to look at Vicki's face, she knew she would think she had lied deliberately, but she had only been thinking of her friend's feelings at the time, now she wasn't sure how this was going to end for their rekindled friendship. "So instead of being honest with me, you sat here and never let on one iota that you and he were shacking up together...that's bullshit Carol and you know it!" she was trying to keep her temper from blowing, "Vicki honestly...I didn't want to cause you anymore upset and I knew telling you would make you mad!" *Feck sake...I don't need this...*Carol wanted this conversation to end, but knowing how angry Vicki was, she knew it was far from over.... "HONESTY! You don't know anything ABOUT BLOODY HONESTY! Otherwise you wouldn't have done this Carol..." aware her voice had risen, Vicki inhaled deeply, "You know he's trouble, I don't understand, why you would want that back in your life, when it's taken a truckload of shit to get it back to some kind of normality from our last encounter with him!" she was hoping reminding her friend of the type of man she was living with would bring her round to her senses. "Vicki, I know exactly what Charlie's like, he's changed...the time he spent inside has changed him and for the better...I mean it!" almost pleading, she had to make Vicki understand that Charlie was no longer the man they had known back then. Just then they heard the banging of the front door, before either could gather themselves, Charlie stood before them.

"Well...Well...What's going on here then?" Charlie asked, curious as to why Vicki was sat in their living room. He could sense an atmosphere, he was certain he was the main reason for it, having heard his name mentioned. "Vicki...isn't it?" he asked her, offering his hand to shake. Vicki stood up from the settee, she did not feel comfortable with this man in the room, never mind him standing over her. *Bloody cheek of him...offering me a handshake...Fecker!* Vicki looked Charlie straight in the eye and refused his offer to shake hands. *As if....hell will freeze over...* The feelings she had for him had not changed throughout the years, although she had to admit to herself, he was still good looking and still carried an air of danger, it was easy to see why Carol had fallen for him. "Let's not kid on, you know it's me...." There was no way she was going to allow him the upper hand here, in any way. "So...to what do we owe the pleasure?" he knew Vicki had no time for him, he understood her distrust of him so there was no point delaying the onslaught of abuse she would fire at him. "Just wondering, why Carol forgot to mention the fact you two are an item, she's telling me you're a changed man and everything's fine, but if that really is the case, then why did she lie about being with you?" She already knew the answer to this, if Carol was so certain he was a changed man she would have told her . Charlie gave a small laugh," I'm new alright.... BRAND NEW... does that make you happy now?" Seething, Vicki grabbed her bag from the floor, "I know YOU'RE trouble! and she'll find out soon enough!" she stated, making her way towards the door. "Vicki! Vicki! Hold on...wait a minute...please Vicki don't go like this" Carol rose from her chair and ran down the hall after her friend, *JEEZUS...I don't need this...*she been feeling tired lately and did not have the strength for anymore drama in her life. Vicki ignored her pleas, and left slamming the door behind her.

This was the last thing he needed, today of all days.

"What'd you have to go and annoy her like that for? You know she needs a bit of time to get her head around us being together, now I might never see her again," cried Carol. "Listen Babe, if she decides you seeing me is enough to call a halt to your friendship, then maybe she wasn't all that great a friend to start with! She'll come back, I guarantee you'll see her again, trust me!" he could tell by the look Vicki had given him as she left, she would be back! Charlie had bigger problems to worry about, mainly, how he was going to get out of this mess with Pete. Going to the park had not helped as much as he had hoped it would. Every time he closed his eyes. he could still see the lifeless body of the girl, this was causing him to lose sleep, to the point he could not see a way out of this nightmare.

CHAPTER NINETEEN

Marching along the landing, satchel swinging at her side, Vicki was so angry and disappointed at Carol. *Stupid cow...bloody deserve each other...*exasperated by her rage, she knew action would need to be taken and she would take it! Out of the corner of her eye she noticed a car approach the parking area below on the Estate, there was something familiar about it. Stopping in her tracks, she leant against the wall on the landing, *What the hell!* She could not believe what her eyes were showing her. Below, getting out of his car was Michael Gold. *OHHH this is interesting, wonder what he's up to*! Keeping her eyes firmly on him, she watched as he made his way up the stairwell opposite from where she stood. Within minutes she saw him exit the stairwell and walk along the second landing, he walked with purpose, her heart fell, as she watched him approach the flat where she had rescued Mandy from.

One knock of the door was all it took before Pete answered.

"What the FUCK is going on here? I've had to put the latest delivery in a safe place...." Growling, Michael entered the flat, "It's stinking in here, and it's not fresh as a feckin' daisy, I thought I told you to make sure this place was cleaned up proper like" he continued, walking from room to room inspecting the place. "Boss, we tried our best, but we're not cleaners, we don't have the right stuff to get this place cleaned proper, don't know what else we could've done" Pete realised the flat was still a mess and not up to the Boss's standards, there was nothing else he could do, he would need to get real cleaners in, at least the blood was off the walls. "What'd you do with Mick? He's a fuckin liability!" Pete followed behind the Boss, "He's sorted for the time being Boss, he won't be talking where he is", after they had disposed of the girls' body, they had come back to the flat where Charlie set about

Mick, at this moment in time he was in a coma in the Western Infirmary. "Good...but I will be catching up with him at some point", Pete knew exactly what the Boss meant by catching up with him, he was glad he was not Mick. "What about this Charlie, can he be trusted?" Michael had not met Charlie, he had been brought on board by Pete, he did not waste time associating with the lackies, that was Pete's job. "Yeah, he's a good guy, don't think we'll have any trouble with him, got too much on him Boss" Pete liked Charlie, his reputation was well known around the town, they had history which he hoped was enough to keep him on board. Michael entered the living room, sat on the chair nearest the door, "Right, here's the plan...."

Outside the weather changed and it began to rain. Vicki had left her umbrella in her car, she got soaked, as she ran from the opposite side of the estate, to the one she had seen Michael in. Well aware of the danger she was placing herself in, she took the stairs two at a time, reaching the landing, she took a deep breath, before walking slowly along in the direction of the flat. *Ohhhhh dear lord, what the hell am I doing?* as she passed the door to the flat, casually peering sideways, trying to find out what was inside, she could not see through the small window, but she could see the door had been busted since her last time here. It was definitely the same flat, where she had found Mandy, as the number six was still clearly showing, on the door. Wary of bringing unwanted attention her way, she walked further along the landing and waited. *You'll need to come out at some point...*she told herself. Time passed slowly as she stood waiting at the end of the landing, just as she was beginning to have doubts about her actions here, the door to the flat opened. Stepping out first was Michael, followed by the man she had seen leave the flat the same day she had found Mandy. Michael turned and locked the door. *Feck sake! What the hell are you up to Michael Gold? ...looks like you're involved in this...I hope not!* Vicki remained glued to the spot, as she watched the two men leave the landing. Michael had the keys to the flat in his hand... *Why does he have the bleeding keys?* They both made their way down the stairwell and onto the Estate below. Once at Michael's car she noticed him pass something to the other man, before he nodded and got into his car. *He's just handed the keys to him...Got you!*

Although Charlie had tried to calm her down and reassure her that she would see Vicki again, Carol was not so sure. Watching him as he slept on the settee she wondered if maybe Vicki was right, perhaps he had not changed. He looked so angelic lying fast asleep, she knew he had not been sleeping properly, especially over the past few weeks. When she enquired as to what was bothering him, he replied that nothing was wrong. This bothered her, she worried he did not trust her, if this was true then she feared for their future, as she knew, if they had no trust then they had no real relationship. Since growing up watching her Mum and Dad argue and fight, Carol always had trust issues with men. Charlie had been an exception, from the moment they had met, she had felt she could trust him. He treated her like a princess and made her feel valued. When she spoke to him, she felt he really listened and cared about the things which were happening in her life. Thinking about those first few weeks, she put her strong feelings down to the fact they had known each other from a traumatic time in both their lives. Sitting reminiscing about their first few weeks together, she could see there was a definite change in his attitude towards her and in his over -all behaviour. Worried for their future, Carol sent up a quick prayer, asking that Charlie be kept safe and trouble free, for the sake of her and their baby....

CHAPTER TWENTY

Arriving back at the office, Vicki went into the small kitchen area, grabbed a hand towel and proceeded to dry herself off. "Get in here...Vicki!" Dougie shouted, from his office, where he sat with PC Young. *Shit! Now what...*she knew he was angry at her for leaving the office on her own earlier, when she debriefed him on her findings it might soften him, she hoped. "Hi David..." she entered the room, carrying a steaming hot cup of coffee, trying to heat herself up. "Hi Vicki, have you got any news for me?" he asked. "As a matter of fact, I have, wait until you hear who I've spotted on the Elton" she replied, as she sat across from the two men.

"Firstly....do any of you remember the name Charlie Sweeney? Dougie you'll recognise the name from my history..." seeing the recognition on Dougie's face, she continued, "Well, he's shacked up with Carol Walker, yeah, another name from my past, and they're both living on the Elton!" Sitting across from her, Dougie raised his eyebrows, digesting this bit of information. "That's not the best bit, during my investigating on the Estate, it's came to my attention that a guy called Michael Gold appears to be involved in the trafficking....but so is Charlie Sweeney!" Feeling smug when she saw the effect of this news on both men, she continued, " I watched two guys with girls go up to that flat, the very same night I witnessed Charlie Sweeney with one of those guys, then today I saw Michael Gold with the same guy, they were at the flat together..." "Whooaa....slow down Vicki...take us back to the very beginning" Dougie was taken aback at the amount of information she had collected, he needed to be sure what she was saying was actually factual and not some figment of her imagination. "Describe the guy you've seen both Charlie and Michael with Vicki" David asked, as he sat further back in his seat. He had heard of Michael Gold, he was known to the Police, but not in the human trafficking business, he was a small fish in the drug business, so he was surprised to find out Vicki had seen him at the flat. Hearing Charlie's name amongst her story did not surprise David. After their meeting in the park and having seen him the night he was on duty, he was expecting him to be involved in some sort of criminal activity on the estate, just not this kind. "He was tall, short fair/ginger hair, well dressed, he had an air of danger about him" Vicki could feel she was onto something big, this was her big story, she just had to join the dots and make the picture clearer. "He's the only one we don't have a name for yet, but I intend to find out who he is and what part he's playing in all this" she felt the excitement build up inside her. The one thing Vicki loved was a challenge, this was proving to be a lot more dangerous than they had first anticipated, yet it was not putting her off, if anything it was making her more determined to get to the truth.

The remainder of the day was spent exchanging details from their individual surveillance sessions. It was becoming more apparent, as the day went on that Charlie and this other guy seemed to be deeply involved, as their names kept coming up with every situation they discussed. David told them about the night he first came back into contact with Charlie. He explained what had happened with the gang members, the manner in which they exchanged greetings. Now I've had a chance to think about his behaviour that night, I think there could be something going on with him, I don't know what yet!" David had thought about Charlie's actions the day in the park, before he had approached him, he seemed preoccupied.

Time passed as the three of them discussed the investigation, between them they decided that David would escort Vicki when she was going onto the Estate. Given the direction it was heading in, they felt this was for the best, the last thing they needed was something happening to her. "Hold on until I grab my bag David," Vicki called, as David walked to the doors. *Bloody men!...* she was annoyed they thought she needed protecting. *If it had not been for my persistence in the first place, you wouldn't have half the info.....*frustration working through her mind, she was beginning to feel resentment towards David. After all, it was down to her hard work, they had most of the details, she'd be damned if PC Plod was going to sweep in and steal her story. Dougie and David both thought it would be a good idea for her to stay close to Carol, use her friendship, as a way of gleaming more information about Charlie. Vicki could see where they were coming from, but the last thing she wanted right now was to see Carol, she was still angry at her for keeping her relationship with Charlie a secret, the only positive she could see, was that this might actually eliminate him from their lives for the last time.

CHAPTER TWENTYONE

The music was loud, and his pint was watery, he was just about to get up from his bar stool when Charlie felt a hand on his shoulder and heard the Irish lilt. "Hey...not so fast Charlie Boy, where you rushing to then?" turning slowly, he saw the hand belonged to Pete McNeil. *Feck sake! What now....* This was the last thing he needed, right at this moment in time. "Just on my way home...had enough of this dump for one night," he replied, feeling more fed up than he had five minutes earlier. *And you can go fuck yourself!* He was in no mood for Pete, it was down to him he was in this mess, he had an idea which would help him, he just had to put it into play. "Easy tiger...why don't you sit down again, and I'll get us both a drink, I think we need a catch up, wouldn't you say...." *Oh! for fucks sake! What the hell's this fucker on about now....* Sitting back down on the bar stool, "If you say so...I'll have a vodka," he said, anticipation building up within him, at what Pete was going to hit him with next!

Several hours later, Charlie headed home, having spent the remainder of his night, sat listening to Pete waffle on about the plan, with the new girls they had taken delivery of, the flat or rather the state of the flat and Mick, who was at present still in his coma, up the Infirmary. Listening to Pete, it had become apparent that he was wanting Charlie to step into Mick's place, since it was mainly due to him, that he was out of the picture at present. Charlie accepted his part in Mick's untimely predicament, although there was a good reason for this, it seemed Pete was more concerned with placing the blame firmly at Charlie's feet, in the hope that the guilt would ensure he played along with his plans. Whilst Pete had rattled on, Charlie's mind switched off. He had plans of his own, although Pete was involved, he would be surprised at the way he fitted in to Charlie's plans.

Sat in his Ford Fiesta, keeping a watchful eye on the people coming and going around the Estate, David was hoping his intended target would make an appearance tonight. He had deliberately told Vicki a small white lie, saying that he had Police business to attend to this evening, therefore being unable to escort her here to the Estate. *If she finds out, she'll be raging...there's a chance she'll not talk to me...* musing this over in his head, he felt bad, he hated being deceitful, but he wanted the opportunity to speak with Charlie Sweeney without her present. He was aware of the history between them both, given the tension between them, he felt it was for the best for the investigation, that he come alone tonight. As he sat turning these thoughts around in his head, he was distracted by a man staggering along the road. David laughed to himself, *someone's obviously had a good night...*chuckling, his eyes following the man's footsteps, swaying from side to side, trying to walk in a straight line. until he recognised who it was. Immediately he stopped laughing at the man's antics, got out of his car and approached Charlie Sweeney.

"Hey there, you look like you could do with some help there, "David stated, putting his hand out to stop Charlie from falling over. He turned too fast to see where the voice had come from, almost lost his balance, "I'm fine mate, just heading up the road..." Charlie mumbled, slanting his eyes, as he struggled to see clearly who it was in front of him. He was alarmed, as he took in the coppers face. David got a strong whiff of alcohol the closer he got to Charlie, *this could work in my favour here...it's now or never...*realising Charlie's senses were dulled due to the effects of the drink, David hoped this would make him more open to his idea. Stepping right in front of him, he stopped Charlie in his tracks, "Charlie, let me help you up to your flat, then maybe we can talk..." he could feel the adrenalin coursing through his body, "I don't need your help!" shouted Charlie, pulling his arm away from the outreached hand. "I think we both know you do..." David stated, taking Charlie's arm and leading up towards the flat.

Fortunately, Carol was spending the night at Tracey's house. When they eventually got into the flat Charlie could feel the effects of the alcohol diminish slightly, he put this down to the company he was in at present. *Christ almighty, I hope there was no-one saw him bring me up here...*he stumbled, walking over to the window, looking down onto the Estate he could not see anyone about, *all quiet...hopefully nobody's noticed there's a fucking copper in here...*panic was setting in now, he closed the curtains over. "Take a seat..." David sat on the chair next to the door, "What makes you think I need your help?" he sneered, sitting on the settee opposite. "This might not be the best time to talk about this, given your state..." David stood up to leave, "Maybe another time Charlie, if you have time that is..." "What the fucks that supposed to mean, if I got time...." David could tell he had struck a nerve, with Charlie jumping on the defence like he had. "I'm only trying to help you out here Charlie, no need to get all heat up, I had an idea you and I could help each other, but maybe another time," he realised he sounded defeated, but David knew he had Charlie's attention. Taking his seat once more, Charlie glared across at him. *He's wondering if he can trust me, I know that's what he's thinking...play the waiting game it'll be worth it...* After what seemed like forever, the tension in the room was thick, he could almost feel it, both men sat deep in their individual thoughts, before Charlie broke the silence. "Right, say we could help one another, what guarantees do I get that I won't end up inside again?" *Bingo!* David gave a silent cheer, preparing a deal in his head that suited them both.

CHAPTER TWENTY-TWO

The constant ring of the telephone awoke Carol from her deep sleep, the first in weeks, as she was worrying about telling Charlie her pregnancy news given his recent behaviour. Reaching across to answer the phone, she almost fell off the settee from where she was lying. *Jeezo...better be bloody worth wakening me.* "Hello....." she answered, " Hi Carol, it's me, Vicki..." she could feel the anxiety building up inside her at hearing Vicki's voice. *What the hell does she want now...*" I was just wondering if you fancied meeting me for a chat and a coffee, I don't want us two falling out..." This was the first time she had heard from Vicki since she had stormed out of her flat after hearing about her relationship with Charlie, "I'm not sure Vicki, I mean I don't want us two falling out either, but I'm not going to end things with Charlie!" "I don't want you to end your relationship Carol, I only want the chance to make it up to you," *God this is bloody hard work...* Vicki knew it wasn't going to be easy making amends with Carol, she remembered how stubborn her old friend was. "Listen, why don't we meet up away from the flat, that might be the easiest solution for us both." Vicki had no intention of seeing Charlie Sweeney, just yet! "Okay then, I'll meet you at the café on the corner of Alexander Street about 2pm?" Carol was not ready to lose her old friend again, *Let's give you one more try...*although she would be wary

Vicki was sat at her desk in the bustling newsroom, replacing the telephone receiver, she was aware of being watched, *that creep Colin's staring again...*swinging around on her chair, there he was, watching her every move. "You alright Colin? Anything I can help you with?" his face reddened, he was caught, "No..No...nothing at all," he replied sheepishly, lowering his head, pretending to be working. Getting up she made her way over to Dougie's office, knocking as she opened the door, "Hey Boss, I've just arranged to meet with Carol, any news from David?" It had been a few days since she had last spoken to David, he had explained he was inundated with official Police work but would try make some time for surveillance work on the Estate. "Nope...nothing at all!" he replied, "Strange, but I suppose his official work has to come first," Vicki had hoped David would have information on the men by now, which would enable the investigation to move forward, it was not moving as quickly as she wanted. "Well, I'll go see what Carol has to say, I'll be in touch," she said, turning and exiting the office, making her way out of the newsroom.

Parking the car, Vicki got out, locked the door and walked towards the café, where she could see Carol, sat at a table near the window. As she walked *Jeezus...she looks ropey*, she was surprised at her friend's appearance, she looked drained, her hair was tied back and greasy looking, her clothes needed an iron run over them. Usually Carol took great care with her appearance, perhaps not her style, but at least looking as though she had washed. "Hi, have you ordered yet?" asking, as she slid into the booth. "No, I was waiting on you, what do you fancy then?" Carol passed her the menu, as the waitress approached to take their orders. Both chose bacon rolls and a cup of tea, Carol praying she would be able to keep it in her stomach, her morning sickness was terrible, she felt lousy today and was aware she looked lousy too.

They enjoyed their breakfast whilst chatting, so far, they had managed to discuss everything from the weather to tv programmes, anything but Charlie! Vicki could see there was something wrong with Carol. Apart from the way she looked, she seemed anxious.... *one of us is going to have to bring him up...here goes.* "So...I think we've dodged the subject as long as we can," she laughed, trying to bring some humour, hoping it might relax Carol. "I don't want to fall out over a guy Carol, we never have, I want to see you happy," Carol sat across from her in the booth, "I am happy, Charlie's been good to me Vicki, I love him and he loves me, I don't want us arguing either," " I'm sorry...Why don't we start again regards Charlie? I can see you have feelings for each other," this was the best Vicki could do, she had to try get Carol to open up to her about her relationship with Charlie. Telling her she was sorry was not ideal to her, but worth it, in order to find out his movements.

"I realise you have feelings for him Carol, I really do, I can't lie, I wish you had never met him again, but maybe I'm just being selfish. Whenever I see him it brings back memories I would rather forget, surely you can understand that?" pleading, she was praying Carol would come to her senses, this was not going to end well for her again. Vicki was struggling not to blurt out the information she had discovered about Charlie. Then again, sitting across from Carol she was not convinced it would make much of a difference to her feelings. "Vicki, I totally see where you are coming from, I was there too, you know what I've been through because of all the trouble he caused in the past, but like I said before, he's changed Vicks...I mean it!" Vicki was only sat across from her, yet there was a distance between them, which felt like they were miles apart. *Maybe if I tell her my news, she'll lay off him a bit...* Carol had not told anyone that she was expecting Charlie's baby, not even him, but she was increasingly feeling under pressure from Vicki, crossing her fingers, she continued," Vicki, please believe me when I say he's not the same man as he was back then, I truly believe we have a good future ahead of us...the three of us..." slowly, she sighed with relief, finally she had told someone, although from the look of confusion on Vicki's face she wasn't sure she had understood what she had just told her. *Bloody hell...has she just hinted she's pregnant by HIM...*this was the last thing she had expected to hear today. "Did you just say the three of you?" she asked, trying hard not to sound as shocked as she felt. "Yeah, I'm pregnant Vicki, I'm having Charlie's baby, we are going to be a family"

Chapter Twenty -Three

Still reeling from Carol's unexpected announcement, Vicki entered her office, walked straight to her desk and threw her bag to the floor and herself into her chair. *What the hell...How could she be so stupid?* Every thought which came into her head was a negative one, she could not for the life of her find anything positive about Carol's news.

When Carol had divulged her news to her in the café, she had nodded whilst trying to hide her shock. Momentarily speechless, Vicki had felt nodding her head, whilst faking a smile, was the best she could offer at the time. Carol was sat across from her, and she could see how anxious she was, she knew she should have been happy for her friend and reassuring her, but as hard as she tried, she just could not find the right words! After dropping Carol off at the Estate, driving back to the office, all Vicki could think about was the impact this news had on her investigation. It was obvious Charlie was involved in the child trafficking ring which she had uncovered. What had also become obvious to her, in meeting Carol, was how serious her relationship with Charlie had become, now with a baby on the way! *Where do I go with this now? How can I ruin her life? I cannot cause her anymore pain...*

"Vicki! are you going to sit there all day?" looking up from her desk, David Young was walking in her direction, she couldn't help noticing how pleased he looked with himself. "Actually! I have not long sat down Sir, so what's with the happy face?" she asked, trying to muster the energy to feel bothered. "OH! I think you're going to like the news I bring to you" he enthused, nodding his head in the direction of Dougie's office. "Come over here and I'll let you into my secret" laughing, he walked ahead of her into the Boss's office. Closing the door behind her, she walked over and sat down next to David, "Right, let's be having it then..." she was in no mood for games, this had better be good! David explained how he had gotten on with Charlie Sweeney. "So, he's definitely on board?" Vicki needed to be one hundred percent certain there was no way he was going to play them. The implications this could have for the investigation were enormous. "He's eighty percent with us, he's obviously scared of the outcome, if the other gang members find out he's passing on information, but... given the fact he's open to working with us is a big deal, don't you agree?" he replied, looking directly at Vicki. "Yeah for sure, but we need him in one hundred and I think I might just have the thing to help push him that bit further in our direction!" The adrenalin was coursing through her body, she could feel the excitement building at the prospect of bringing down the gang, this was going to boost her career in the world of journalism. Somewhere in the back of her mind, there was a BUT what about Carol moment, she had not yet told Charlie he was going to be a Father, yet the realisation that her dreams could become a reality was too strong for her to turn her back on! " I met with Carol today and she has informed me that she's carrying Charlie's baby...perhaps he would be willing to help us more if he realised he was going to become a Daddy." Both men gave her a bewildered look, "Right, look at his background...he was adopted, this was the catalyst which brought him into our worlds the first time, so...I don't think he would want any child of his growing up without him!" Dougie sat nodding, eventually seeing what she was saying, "I think you could have something there, Miss!"

"Any news on Mick yet?" he asked Pete, not that he was worried for his general health, but he needed to keep an eye on him. Michael knew from past experiences, that he could not trust Mick from opening his mouth if the Old Bill should come sniffing about. "He's still in a coma Boss, don't think he'll be causing us trouble anytime soon!" Pete was eager to settle the Boss's nerves, if he was feeling edgy it only meant more aggro for him, something he could be doing without. "The new dark haired one in the Elton flat, she ain't bringing me in much business, get rid of her. I'll get another girl from another flat brought over, better to keep a pair in there" he was getting grief from the hierarchy. Losing a girl, then Mick killing one, meant that they had come to the attention of the Romanians and they were not happy! It was up to him to prove that they still had a hold on this side of the business. Michael was struggling, he felt under pressure, he was losing control of things around him. *I need some fun, wonder what Vicki's up to?* he pondered, as he dialled the telephone.

Chapter Twenty- Four

Charlie stood watching from the living room window, across at the flat he witnessed Pete and some other guy he had not seen before escort another young girl inside to a life of misery. *What's that Fucker up to now?* As far as he was concerned the flat already had two girls working from it, he was puzzled, as to why there was another one being taken in. Since his conversation with PC Young, he had been keeping a low profile, doing enough to keep Pete off his back. The last thing he wanted was to be dragged into more shit, if he was going to help the Old Bill then he couldn't afford it! Although he was still unsure about becoming an informer, he knew deep down what was going on across in that flat was sickening. Yet he feared for his life and Carol's, if they ever found out it was him feeding the information, they would kill them both without a second's hesitation.

"Hey Babe, you got my dinner on?" Carol called from the front door, returning home from work. Kicking off her shoes, she walked down the hallway into the living room, where she found her man looking out of the window. "Hey Babes, did you hear me?" she approached Charlie from behind, placing her arms around his waist, she snuggled into his back. "Yeah! Yeah! I heard you" he lied, he had been miles away in his mind! Turning, he took her in his arms, giving her a strong hug, "Oh watch Babes, you'll squash me" she laughed, disengaging herself from his hold. *This might be the best time to tell him*, she thought, "Why don't we sit down over here," guiding him towards the settee, "I've got something I need to tell you..." She could see the change in his face, "It's nothing to worry about...well I don't think it is..." she tried to reassure him, as they both sat face to face on the settee. "Feck sake Carol...what's going on?" he could feel the anxiety build up inside him. Taking hold of his hands in hers, "I'm pregnant Charlie! We're going to be a Mummy and Daddy!" Charlie's face lit up with happiness, relief surged through Carol's body. "Are you sure? I mean have you seen a Doctor or done a test?" excitement was building up inside him, this was the last thing he expected, but it was good news, as far he was concerned, he was going to have HIS own family! "Yes! I'm sure Babes!" The rest of the evening Charlie hardly thought about the flat across the estate, he was too busy talking about the baby and making plans for their future together, the three of them!

*I'm off my head! Maybe I should've told David or Dougie where I was going...*Vicki was beginning to doubt herself. When she had answered the telephone earlier, she was surprised to hear Michael Gold on the other end. It had been a few weeks since she had last spoken to him, less time had passed since she had witnessed him on the Elton Estate. Walking to the pub where they had agreed to meet, she was full of trepidation. Although they had known each other from their youth, his recent behaviour had shown her that she didn't really know him at all! Entering the pub, she looked around to see if he had arrived. Looking around nervously, she spotted him sitting at a table situated right in the corner. *A nice and quiet place for a chat or to threaten someone...*she took a deep breath. "Hi Michael, have you been waiting long?" she asked, pulling out the chair to take a seat. "No, not too long, you're worth the wait!" he replied laughing, *Oh my God, he's such a creep*! "Yes, well it has been quite a while since our last catch up", he stood up, pushing the chair back, "What would you like to drink?" he asked her, "Mmm... Think I'll have a vodka and coke please", he smiled, as he made his way towards the bar. *This is going to be a long night....* she let out a large sigh!

The rest of the evening felt like a game of cat and mouse, each one for a different reason. Michael was trying his best to charm her, he could not understand why she was blowing hot and cold with him. One minute she was acting interested in him, asking him all sorts of questions, he thought she was really into him. When he asked her questions about her life and friends, she shut up and reverted it back to him, this was a whole new level of playing hard to get, but he wasn't one for giving up!

Meanwhile Vicki was becoming more frustrated by the minute! It was clear he had no idea what she knew, the more she asked, the more he expected in return. *This is harder than I thought*...having to sit and pretend she was genuinely into him, was slowly draining the life out of her. Sure, he was being responsive to her charms, just not providing anything she could work with regards the investigation. She watched him go to the bar for another round of drinks, *how can he be so charming, yet have this air of danger I didn't notice before?*

Next morning Vicki lay in her bed thinking about the previous night. Michael had not given her any fresh information, which might help with her investigation. He was throwing back the drinks, she hoped this might loosen his tongue, unfortunately it had not done so. At the end of the night he asked her back to his place, she might have considered this before she knew of his underhand dealings. During their meeting in the pub she still felt the odd flutter in her stomach, he was a handsome, sexy man and he was trying his hardest to charm her into his bed. Vicki had to constantly remind herself of the reason she was there in the first place. *Just my luck, I find someone I like and he's a madman! Bloody typical*...she could have kicked herself! "Vicki are you staying in bed all day?" her Mum called to her, as she poked her head around her bedroom door. Vicki pulled the covers over her head, wishing she could lay here in the safety of her bed forever, but she had to tell David and Dougie what she had done last night, something she was not looking forward to, as she knew they would be annoyed with her to say the least.

"Tell us you are joking Missy!" Dougie's face was red with rage. "No! I met with him to see if I could get more information, see if he would slip up..." she nervously answered her Boss. "Yeah because he was just going to admit to you that he's forcing under-age girls into sex, for God's sake Vicki, wake up and smell the bleeding coffee! The main thing is you placed yourself in danger, he might have found out we are on to him, what would you have done then?" Never in her time at The Daily had she seen her Boss this angry. *He's going to take me off this case...* "Boss, I realise I took a chance meeting up with him, but it was in a public place, If he thought I was onto him, there's no way he would've met me, he was only interested in getting me into his bed" Dougie raised his eyebrows, "No I did not! Before you ask! You know I'm not as daft as you might think I am..." she took a deep breath, trying to calm herself down, it was part anger at his insinuation, part fear of being removed from the case. "Go back to your desk Vicki, AND don't think about leaving this office today!" quickly, she got up from her seat and headed towards her desk, feeling like a she'd had a lucky escape!

Busily writing up her notes on the case, she was disturbed by the shouting coming from Dougie's office. Looking over, she could see him pacing up and down his room, he was very animated as he continued talking loudly, with whoever was on the other end of the speaker phone. Looking over in her direction, he signalled for her to come over to his office before she could quickly look away. *Jeezo, what has happened now?* Nervously, she entered the room. Dougie was ending the call, "Right ...right, well find out and get back to me asap!" Walking around his desk, he took a seat across from her. "That was David Young, they've found another young girl...dead!" Shocked, Vicki did not know how to respond to this new information, it was obvious from Dougie's shouting he was angry and frustrated, at the loss of another young life. "When? Where did they find her?" she had so many questions she wanted to ask. "Apparently, it was some old man came across her body at the side of the woods, left lying like a piece of rubbish Vicki, we need to get these Bastards before they take another one!" Never had she witnessed her Boss so upset and angry about a case, probably due to the fact it was young girls and he had daughters himself, a bit too close to home as well. "Have they any leads? Witnesses?" hoping he would tell her the Police had positive lines of enquiry, "Nothing! Bloody usual...how can some piece of shit dump a body, and no-one sees a thing? I'm telling you Vicki, we are not stopping until those pieces of scum are behind bars!" Vicki could not agree more with that statement.

Chapter Twenty-Five

Revelling in the knowledge he was to become a Dad, Charlie felt as though he was going to burst with the excitement of having his own family. When Carol had told him, she was nervous about breaking the news, he could understand her thinking. They had not been together long, he had not really let his barriers down with Carol, so he was not surprised to hear her say this. Yet this was the best thing to happen in his life. Deep down, the thought of having his own kids, the love and security of his own family, was the one thing Charlie dreamt about, he never believed it would become his reality one day. He had made a promise to Carol and himself, that he would put their family's future before anything else in the world!

Opening the front door and finding Pete standing in front of him, was enough to bring Charlie back to earth with an almighty bang!

"Alright mate, thank fuck you're in, I need your help..." Pete stated, walking straight into Charlie's flat. Charlie followed him into his living room, his anxieties rising higher by the minute. "What's going on? Is it Mick?" he was expecting to hear of Mick's passing, as he had been in the coma for ages, "Nah, he's still the same mate, I wish it was him..." trickles of sweat showed on Pete's forehead, causing Charlie to fear what was going to come out of his mouth next. "Well, what the fucks up with you then, you're in some state man?" Pete began shaking his head from side to side, "It was never meant to get like this, I never wanted to get this involved mate...You know we changed the girls across the road, well it was the Boss's idea..." Charlie nodded, as he sat on the edge of the chair whilst Pete continued to walk around the living room. "He told me I had to get rid of the one we were taking out of the flat...I mean RID, You... know what I'm saying?" he asked Charlie, glaring at him, "I did, but now the fucking Old Bill have found the body! Mate...I'm not going back inside!" The desperation was clear to hear in Pete's voice, he sounded like a man on the edge.

Unsure, as to what Pete was expecting him to do, Charlie tried to hide his shock at the horrors Pete divulged to him, explaining how the young girl's death had come about. "You'll need to try lay low for a while Mate, that's the only thing you can do...." Probably not helping Pete to calm down by stating the obvious, it was the best Charlie could offer! "Listen Pete, my Missus is due back any minute, she sees the state of you, she'll start asking questions...I think it's best you leave, and I'll meet you later, eh?" The last thing Charlie wanted right now was to cause Carol any stress or cause for concern. If he could get Pete out of the flat, it would give him some time to think through his options with this information. "Ok, I hear you Mate, I just don't know how this is going to go...." Pete headed off the direction of the front door, relief flooded through Charlie's body, "I know ...I know, we can have a think, see where we go from here...." he thought he sounded sincere, *Christ sake, I almost believed myself there*! Closing the door behind him, he went into the bedroom, threw himself on the bed, and lay planning a way in which, he could make this work for himself and HIS future!

Knocking of the door, once more, *Who the hell is this now? it better not be him again...* he got up, opened the door, surprised for the second time at who stood before him*! Uch shit, last thing I need....* Standing in front of him was Vicki Carey!

"Carol's not in!" he stated, slowly closing the door in her face. "It's actually you I've come to see!" came her reply. Taken aback at her admission, "How come? You can't stand me.... You've made that clear," he was not in the mood for Vicki or her trying to cause him more aggro. "I think we need to have a chat, it's about Carol!" This got his attention, opening the door, he allowed her into the flat. Inside Vicki followed Charlie along to the living room, "You can sit down if you want," he said, pointing towards the settee. "Thanks", she replied, as she sat across from him. The atmosphere in the room was thick with animosity, "So what's the big thing about Carol?" He wanted Vicki out of his house as soon as possible, they both disliked one another and were not good at hiding it! "Well, the thing is...I met up with her the other day, she told me something and I think you need to be aware of it, because I don't want you hurting her...." Charlie stood up abruptly, "Whoa...wait a minute you! Who the hell do you think you are, coming here to my house, telling me how I should be treating my girlfriend, You've some neck on you Vicki Carey!" This was the reaction she was expecting from him, *See.... still the same fly off the handle Charlie Sweeney!* she smirked to herself. "I'm trying to look out for my friend! From your reaction she needs it, you have not changed one bit...still the same hot head as before. You're not kidding anyone especially me!" Anger building up inside her, Vicki inhaled deeply, in an effort to gain some composure back. "Look, you and I don't like each other, that's obvious for the world to see, but we both have an interest in Carol, so can we at least calm it, for her sake, because she's going to need us both in the future..." Charlie stared at her in disbelief, "You know...don't you? About the baby...she's told you first!" She could hear the hurt in his voice, "Yeah, I know! Carol let it slip, she didn't mean to tell me, we were arguing...about you actually...she said it before she realised," he turned away, looking out of the window into the Estate below. *Shit, I need to turn this around, he's never going to help me now...*Vicki looked calm on the outside, however, inside she was panicking. "Charlie, listen...I know it's not what you wanted...me finding out about the baby before you, but the main thing is there is a baby, you and Carol are going to have a family. Surely that's the important thing," turning from the window, he looked at her and shrugged his shoulders. "Carol's over the moon at the thought of your future, all the exciting times ahead of you both, maybe you should focus on that too," walking towards her, he sat down on the edge of the settee, "Ok I suppose the main thing is the baby, well you've made sure I know now, so you can leave!" His feelings were hurt, he could not deny it, but he WAS going to become a Dad and that's all that mattered to him.

"There's something else..." *Here goes nothing...*Vicki was hesitant, "I am working on a case at the moment and your name has come up!" *There said it! This is it!* She was slightly scared of the reaction she was going to get, given how he had erupted earlier. This was dangerous territory she was moving into, they both knew that. Standing in front of her, Charlie stared at her for several minutes before he answered, "What are you talking about? I ain't involved in nothing shady, even if I was, it'd have nothing to do with you!" she was getting well under his skin today. *She had better keep her feckin nose out!* He did not need this today at all! "We both know that's not true Charlie! I'm not asking to cause you more trouble, I'm asking because I can help you! If you'll let me, we could help each other!" nervously, she watched him, unmoved, giving nothing away. Anticipation was in the air, they both realised they could help each other, it was a waiting game to see who was going to bend first. *I'm going to have to divulge some information for him to believe me...* "I know that there are girl's being kept in a flat across the Estate, young girls, I also know one disappeared!" he flinched, "I don't know anything about any flat or girls'...you're barking up the wrong tree here..." he could feel his anxieties building up inside. *Keep it cool, she knows nothing else, she's clutching at straws...*moving over to the chair, Charlie took a seat. "Charlie, this is not going to go away, as much as you can try and deny it...I know your involved, I don't think you're in too deep, but deep enough to be sent back inside. Surely, that's the last place you want to be heading, especially with the baby on the way...we can help each other, this is a chance for you to put yourself and your family first," He was listening intently to what she had to say, she continued relaying all the information she had about the girls' and the flat. *Fuck! She has been doing her homework...*

When Vicki had finished informing him of the knowledge she had learned, he felt he had no choice but to work with her. "Right, but before we go any further, I need reassurances here...You need to promise me that my name is kept out of this!" Although she had PC Young on her side, Vicki was not sure how the Police would feel about her making false promises. "There's no way I can promise you that, all I can do is ensure the Police are aware that you have helped us, I'm sure that will go a long way in keeping you out of jail," hoping he could not hear the desperation in her voice, she was silently praying that he was not going to back out of this opportunity for himself and Carol. "Have you got anyone in the Old Bill working with you?" There was no chance he was giving her anything until he felt sure she was the real deal, "I have actually, there's an Officer we both know, he's been helping me with surveillance and stuff" she did not want to blow David's cover, yet she knew she had to tell Charlie something solid in order for him to believe she meant business. Charlie thought of PC Young and the conversation they had shared about working together. *This is all beginning to add up...I bet she's talking about the same Copper...*

Chapter Twenty-Six

Feeling enthusiastic and motivated, Vicki walked straight into Dougie's office, "Hey Boss, wait until you hear about my day, this is going to blow you away..." flinging her satchel to the ground, she grabbed the chair, pulled it out from under his desk and fell into it. She had been emotionally drained after leaving Charlie, yet the more she thought about the implications this could have for the investigation and her career, the more excited she had become driving back to the office. Now she had Dougie's full attention, "I've just come from having a chat with Charlie Sweeney...." Dougie's eyes grew open wide, "You don't need to worry, it was a chance, I know, but it has paid off big Boss! He's agreed to help us catch they pieces of scum that murdered the girl!" Across the desk, Dougie sat surprised, "Two things...Firstly, I told you to stay away from him, unless you were with someone! Secondly...How did you get him to agree with this plan of yours?" he knew there was no point in arguing with her, she was going to do her own thing, no matter what he said to try and stop her. Dougie hoped it would not be to her detriment.

Having relayed the information to Dougie, she was feeling pleased with herself. They decided to wait until they had updated David with this new development before deciding the best way to move forward. Charlie had explained to her about his meeting with David, how he had reservations at the time, although he still felt uneasy, he was willing to involve himself now. Vicki felt certain that David would appreciate this fact, just maybe not the way she had gone about it!

Sitting at the bar, Pete downed another straight whiskey, feeling the warmth it caused as it glided down his throat. "Put another in there! Keep them coming!" he instructed the barman. "Slow down there..." came a voice from behind him. Pete recognised the voice straight away, he turned to find Michael Gold standing alone. *Fuck sake*! This was the last person he wanted to see tonight, he was sitting here waiting on Charlie showing his face. "Are you having a party for one here? Or have you got some problems you're trying to forget?" Michael had made the journey across town, because he had not been able to get a hold of the man sat in front of him. *He doesn't look good, this better not mean trouble for me!* He deliberated, given the state Pete was in and the fact he had been avoiding him! "Here, why don't we go and sit somewhere a bit more private, catch up proper like...." Dread coursing through him, Pete slid from the bar stool and followed in his Gaffer's footsteps towards a table in the corner of the pub. "So, is everything ok with you then?" asked Michael, checking him up and down. He had to admit, he had seen him look better. "I've been trying to get in touch, it's almost as though you're not wanting me to find you.... I'm struggling here, not to take it personal!" Pete heard the menace in Michael's words, it made him feel more on edge, "As if Gaffer....I've just had some personal stuff to deal with, you know what it's like...with the missus and kids," Michael wasn't even aware Pete had a wife or kids, he had never heard him mention either before, for all he knew they did not exist. He always went with his gut instinct, at this moment it was telling him Pete was lying!

Charlie entered the pub, he looked over to the bar, Pete was usually sat there, keeping the bar staff busy. There was no sign of him at his usual seat, *Thank Feck, he's not here!* Feeling relieved, he turned, heading in the direction of the exit, when out of the corner of his eye, he saw Pete sitting, looking nervous with a guy he did not recognise. *Feck sake! Who the feck is that?* Charlie's first instinct was to run out of the door, as fast as he could, yet, he found himself walking over towards Pete and the unknown male.

"Hey Pete, there you are man!" both heads turned towards him, it was clear to see the relief wash over Pete at his arrival to the table. This unsettled Charlie, if Pete was nervous with this guy, then this was someone serious. Pete McNeil was not the type who scared easily! "Hey Charlie, you made it! So glad you decided to join me mate" said Pete, getting to his feet, "What are you drinking then?" he asked, walking over to the bar before he could reply. Charlie followed behind him, "Whoa…wait a minute, I've not even told you what I want…." Pete was at the bar staring straight ahead, "We need to get out of here! Don't look round, that's the Gaffer!" both men stood looking in the mirror behind the bar, watching as The Gaffer finished his drink.

Charlie? Michael was sure he had heard Pete talk about 'a Charlie' doing some work for them. Therefore, he did not think he had anything to worry about with the arrival of this guy.

"How do you suggest we get out of here, he's watching us!" Charlie wished he had acted on his gut instinct and left when he had first seen Pete at the table. Pete turned to see Michael staring over at them, he gestured the drinks were on him over to Michael, who nodded his agreement for another one. "Stick with me Charlie! Do not leave me alone with him!" Pete stated, as the barman headed in their direction. "You owe me for this Pete!" he replied, as long as he kept his mouth shut and listened, this could work in his favour.

Vicki lay in the bath, enjoying the heat easing her aching muscles and the smell of the lavender bubble bath relaxing her mind. After the day she had endured, her body was wracked with tension, this was exactly what she needed. Everything was falling into place regards the investigation. David Young had popped into the office later that afternoon, which was ideal, it had given her the chance to debrief him about her visit to Charlie. He was cautiously optimistic that they would secure arrests and put an end to the trafficking in their area. All they had to do was hope Charlie would keep to his end of the deal.

Chapter Twenty-Seven

The smell of bacon greeted Charlie's senses, as he woke from a disturbed night's sleep. As much as he had tried to fall asleep, he tossed and turned most of the night.

What he had heard discussed last night in the pub with Pete and Michael Gold disturbed him, even more so than he was previously! They were seriously upping their game, bringing in more young girls and boys now! Michael had instructed Pete to find more flats, in order to place the new 'goods', he was also told he needed to find more guys to make sure there was at least two in every flat. "Don't want another fuck up like the one that dick had caused" were his exact words, he was referring to Mick and the girl.

Meeting Michael Gold for the first time, he was surprised that he was 'The Gaffer' which Pete kept referring to. In Charlie's mind he had pictured someone big and tough looking, but what he found was a smart looking, clean shaven, business type guy. Nothing near what he had envisioned at all! Although he had to admit, he did carry an air of danger about him, Charlie could see why Pete chose to stay on his good side. The details of the expected delivery of new 'goods' were put in place last night. He was apprehensive about sharing them, in-case they found out he was the one informing the coppers. He did not need to use much of his imagination, to see exactly how he would be dealt with, this terrified him, the thought of his unborn baby was the only reason he was taking his chances.

"That's them ready Charlie," Carol called through from the kitchen. Jumping out of the bed, he stepped into his jeans and followed the smell of bacon sandwiches through to where Carol was sat at the table. "Have you got anything planned for today Babes? You didn't get much sleep last night, you okay?" enquired Carol. Due to him moving about in the bed, she had hardly slept herself, she was tired this morning but had agreed to cover a shift at the store. "Yeah, I'm fine, probably the drink to blame, when are you due at your work?" Thinking they might have time to go back to bed, sex always helped him when he was stressed, he could certainly be doing with relaxing right now! "Not due in until lunch time...." She saw the glint in his eyes, "Come on then..." grabbing his hand, they ran back to the comfort of their bed and each other.

Sunday mornings were Vicki's favourite! The long lie in bed, then planning the day ahead. Sometimes she stayed home, especially if she had been out the night before with Amber. The thing she loved most about Sundays were having the choice, with no work she could do whatever she fancied. Going out, whether it be to the market in the town or a drive to the coast. This always helped clear her mind, it was good for setting her up for the week ahead.

Feeling she needed some fresh air and to clear her mind, she decided on a drive to the beach. *Yip, the sound of the waves and some sea air, just what I need!* Throwing back the covers, she quickly washed and dressed. "Mum...I'm going out, I'll grab something to eat when I get there!" she said, making her way down the hallway, towards the front door "Wait! There was someone called David on the phone for you earlier. I did not want to waken you, because You would've moaned!" Stopping dead in her tracks, she turned, retracing her steps back up the hallway, "What time was that he called? Did he say why?" her Mum was sitting in her usual spot, in front of the television. "About nine this morning... and No, he didn't say why he was phoning so early on a Sunday morning. It's a good job I was already up, or he would've got a piece of my mind!" Normally, her Mum would've been still asleep, "Why are you up so early? Are you feeling okay?" aware this could be taken as cheek, "I mean usually you like a long lie as well..." looking at her Mum, she looked fine, but this did not stop her worrying. "I'm fine, I'm going into Town to meet James, we're going to the car boot sale, we want to be there early, catch the best bargains. No need to worry about me!" Vicki knew her Mum had been fed up sitting in herself lately, she was feeling bad, because she was spending so much of her time working on this case. "Aww that's great, you'll enjoy searching for the treasures, the two of you," glad that James had invited Mum along, it took some of the guilt she was feeling away, knowing her Mum was not left indoors alone, again. "I'll see if I can get a hold of David, maybe..." her Mum cut in before she could finish her sentence, "HE left his number, said you've to call as soon as you can!" she watched her Mum get up off the armchair, walk into the hallway, she lifted a piece of paper from the top of the telephone. "Here, who is he anyway? Your latest Boyfriend?" *If only it was that simple...* "No! he's not actually, he's a work colleague" she replied curtly, lifting the receiver, she dialled David's number.

They agreed to meet at the old bandstand in the park. Given it was a Sunday and it was a nice day outside, the park would likely be busy with people taking advantage of a good day. They would not look out of place, a nice couple out for a romantic stroll...instead they were planning to take down a sex trafficking ring.

"So, Charlie called you last night, straight after leaving them?" disbelief, in her voice. "Yes, he said he had to tell me right away, he was honest Vicki, said if he went home and thought about what he was doing... then chances were, he wouldn't tell us at all! He sounded shaken," It almost sounded as though David was pleading his case, "I am surprised that he was so willing to give you details, surely you must be too," shaking his head, "No, not really, I think you are missing the point, you're forgetting how much this baby means to him, he is serious about not going back to jail and the info he has provided, well... I feel has proven this," They walked side by side through the tree lined pathway, "Right! Let's hear what he had to say then,"

"Well, he went to The Stag's Head pub to see Pete McNeil; that's the guy you already know from the flat, apparently, he had turned up at Charlie's door asking for his help. It turns out it was this Pete character that murdered the young girl we found last week." Vicki looked up at him, mouth agape, "Wait, let me finish," he could see she was dying to ask more questions, "Charlie told him he would see him later in the pub, he was scared in case Carol came home to find them talking, he does not want her involved. So later, he walks into the pub to find Pete in the company of the head honcho..." he put his hand out to indicate she should stay quiet, whilst he continued, "He wasn't expecting anyone else to be there, turns out neither did Pete. This guy they call 'The Gaffer' had turned up out of the blue, he was looking all over for Pete, because he had gone to ground, he's terrified of this guy." He stopped for a breath, "They're expecting a new shipment of 'goods' as they call them. This time it's girls and boys, they're branching out, big time Vicki!" Vicki stood shocked in front of him, "So, this 'Gaffer'...Do we have a name for him?" David gave a nod of his head, "Yeah, it's Michael Gold, the small time drug dealer, never would I have thought he'd be into this, never mind running it!" as he spoke, he watched the colour drain from Vicki's face, "Are you feeling alright Vicki, here sit down, you've gone very pale!" gently, he helped her down to sit on the grass. It felt as though hours passed before she could use her voice, although it was a few minutes, "Michael Gold...he's the one running this? Are you sure?" totally overcome by disbelief and shock! Vicki felt as though she had been hit by a brick to the head, she was glad David was sat on the grass next to her, "Yes! That's the name Charlie gave me, I'm certain. Why would you doubt this, he's already in the system, he's a piece of work," David was slightly bewildered at Vicki's reaction, "Do you know him?" he asked, Vicki nodded her head, as she looked across at him. "I've was seeing him...but it's apparent I don't know him!" admitting this, made her feel stupid. "Seeing him? As in romantically?" her admission surprised him, "How could I have spent time with him and all the while he's been running this. How did I not see this?" frustration building up inside her, she was more determined than before. *Well, I'll make sure it's the last time you trick me, Michael Gold!*

Chapter Twenty-Eight

Once back in the sanctuary of her house, Vicki went straight to her bedroom. The noise coming from up the hallway, told her that James and her Mum, were back from their treasure hunt at the car boot sale. Longing to be left on her own, she closed the bedroom door, crept into bed and underneath her covers. *How the hell could I have missed this?* The question had whizzed about her mind, since hearing David mention Michael's involvement in their enquiry. Under the covers Vicki began to cry, feeling betrayed, this case had become personal to her now! They had decided to leave any further debriefing until the next morning, they arranged to meet at the office, to tell Dougie of their latest findings.

The next morning Vicki still felt betrayed by Michael Gold, throughout the night she kept going back to the time she had seen him at the flat on the estate. Telling herself she should have confronted him, instead of ignoring her gut instinct at the time. *Bloody stupid! Maybe I could have done something earlier, stopped more girls becoming used...*This guilt was beginning to eat away at her, she realised she needed to act fast, in order to prevent his grand plan from coming into fruition, and she vowed that she would!

Quickly she got showered and dressed, grabbed her satchel from her bedroom floor and ran to her car. The rain was pouring down this morning, it suited her mood. On arriving at 'The Daily' office, she was the first in, she went over to the kitchen area to put the kettle on, she needed her morning coffee, it always eased her into the day ahead. "Good on yourself Vicki, I'll have one too!" shouted Dougie, walking towards his office. Vicki had not heard him enter the room, her mind was miles away, trying to make sense of everything which had happened between herself and Michael Gold. *How could I have missed this?* Was the question on repeat in her mind! Finished making the coffees, she turned to find David heading through the doors. "I suppose you want a one as well?" she asked, holding up the mugs. "You read my mind, yes that'll be great Vicki, is he in yet?" he enquired, looking in the direction of Dougie's office. "Yes, not long in...let me get your drink, then we can go tell him the good news," replied Vicki.

After a long debrief, Dougie made the decision that they would keep the information to themselves, for the time being. He felt there was more to come from Charlie, which would give them a better story. This was not sitting well with David, but he was outnumbered, they had tried to reassure him. Reluctantly, David agreed to go ahead with the plan in place. "I'm not going to pretend this is sitting easy with me, it goes against everything I stand for. I am supposed to be looking out for vulnerable people, keeping them safe, not allowing them to suffer more...," Vicki heard the angst in his voice, "We realise that David, but as long as Charlie's in there for us, we will know first hand if they will be in anymore danger, won't we?" aware she was sounding desperate. This story was going to take her career beyond catastrophic! All her years as a trainee journalist, she had dreamt about breaking a story of this magnitude. It was going to happen now, she would not allow anyone to stand in her way! As she was leaving Dougie's office, she watched a delivery guy with a large bunch of red roses approach Colin at his desk. "OH! Colin has a secret admirer!" she laughed, walking towards her desk. "Actually, they're for a Miss Carey, and I am not she!" Colin's attempt at humour was lost on her. He waved the delivery guy in her direction, "He needs a signature"

Vicki signed for the flowers, "Hurry up then, reveal your admirer" It was David who had come up from behind her, he was so close she could feel his breath on her neck. "Wait a minute," her hands had begun to shake, not sure whether with excitement or fear, she opened the envelope, "What the hell!" she threw the card into the waste paper bin at the side of her desk. "Who are they from?" David asked as he bent down to retrieve the card from the bin. "Love Michael xx" David read the card aloud, "Someone thinks he's still in with a shout Vicki" Dougie appeared at her desk, "What's all this commotion about?" his eyes landing on the roses. "Who sent them?" Vicki and David both looked at him, "I think we need to go into your office Boss," she did not want Colin to hear anything. Once the three of them were back in Dougie's office, she closed the door. "Michael Gold has sent them!" she stated, Dougie could see how visually shook up she was, "Do you think he knows we are onto him? It's just weird, they turn up today of all days..." guiding her to take a seat, "When was the last time you were in his company?" Dougie asked, "Not that long ago, he has not been in touch since the night he was drunk," "Well, perhaps he's sending them as a way of apology, for acting like an arse" this time it was David trying to calm her fears. "There's no way he knows anything about our enquiries, calm down and take them as they are meant ...a way of saying sorry for being drunk!" Nodding her head, she stood up and went across to her desk. Lifting the flowers, she placed them in the bin. "Best place for them and him!"

Across town in his office, Michael Gold lay back on his chair, with his feet upon his desk, feeling smug with himself. *I hope she likes her delivery!*

Chapter Twenty-Nine

Carol and Charlie had been for their weekly shopping. Charlie met her at work every Friday, they bought their groceries and Carol used her discount card, to try save some money. They would need every penny, especially with the baby on the way. Walking along the street next to the Estate, a car rolled up alongside them. Charlie bent to see inside, as the window began lowering, "Feck sake man, you trying to give us a heart attack here?" he called to Pete, who was driving the car. The car came to a halt, "Jump inside I'll give you a lift" leaning across the passenger's seat to open the door, "Nah, your alright mate, we are nearly there, I'll catch you later!" Charlie tried hard to keep his two worlds apart from each other. The less Carol knew or was involved the better for them all. "Suit yourself, meet me in the Stag in an hour!" then he drove off, with the tyres screeching. Dread filled Charlie, he hated what Pete had him involved in, but he accepted it was himself to blame. Every night he prayed for it all to come to an end. He was feeling the pressure from both sides and now Carol was asking questions, "What's he wanting to meet you for?" Carol suspected he was up to no good, "Is that not the same guy from that night in the pub?" she never gave him the chance to answer. "I'm sure it is, you had better not be up to anything dodgy Charlie!" rolling his eyes, "Don't be daft Babe, I told you before, he'll just be after some advice, women problems or something like that," he hoped this was enough to stop her curiosity.

Sitting on his favourite stool at the bar, Pete's nerves were beginning to get the better of him. Until recently he felt self- assured and confident, he was in control and he was enjoying the money which he was earning. Suddenly, he was longing to be free of the responsibility of running this area for 'The Gaffer'. Ever since the night he had dropped by to tell him they were expanding the business, Pete felt unsettled. Perhaps it was the fact he had not been asked his opinion on the expansion. After all, he was the one left with the day to day running of the area. Any problems, it was left up to him to get them sorted, either personally or know someone who could. He felt 'The Gaffer' was beginning to take liberties and he wasn't having that!

"Alright Mate," seeing Charlie helped calm his nerves. He knew he could always rely on him for support in these matters. "Yeah, fine, so what's the problem?" he asked, as he sat on the stool next to him. "Get a couple of drinks in, we'll talk over there," replied Pete, pointing over to a corner table. *AHHHH! What the Feck now?* Charlie really was not in the mood for this today. This morning he was looking forward to getting the shopping with Carol, then spending the rest of his day relaxing, just him and her! He had promised Carol he would not be out long. Carrying the two pints of lager over to the table, Pete took a large gulp, "I needed that!" wiping the corners of his mouth. "I think you've already had quite a few Mate, what's up?" it was obvious from the state Pete was in there was something bothering him. "It's 'The Gaffer, I feel like he's taking the piss Mate," Charlie tried to hide his surprise, this was not what he was expecting from Pete. "What do you mean? I thought you two were sorted, it sounded that way the other night," Charlie was confused, they had acted like best buddies, Pete had sat agreeing with everything that was put forward. "He's piling the pressure on mate, I don't like being told what to do and when to do it! I realise he's getting it from the Romanian side, but I'm in charge on my own patch Charlie!" beads of sweat were on Pete's forehead, "Well, don't let him see you like this man! Has he changed his mind since the other night?" Charlie had to be sure he was sharing the correct details with the old bill and Vicki. "Nah, it's me...he's wanting to get rid of more used goods, because the new ones coming in. I need your help Charlie!"

Walking home, Charlie's mind was racing! Pete's request had shocked him. The plan was for them to make room, in order to bring in more girls and boys, Charlie was definitely not going to be doing away with anyone, he had made this clear to Pete. He had left him sitting alone in the pub drinking himself into oblivion. As far as he was concerned, he had done his bit, when he had helped Pete hide the body of the girl Mick had murdered. Charlie's anxiety was building inside him, he was way out of his depth here, he had to inform his contacts of the new plans, they would need to act fast, if there were to be no more bodies!

Monday morning commute to work was always busy. Vicki decided to make a detour to Carol's place, she had not seen her for a while. Driving onto the Estate, she noticed there were more cars than normal. Shrugging this observation off, she made her way up the smelly stairwell onto Carol's landing. Glancing across the Estate from this height, she got a different perspective. The door to the flat where the girls were housed opened. Vicki witnessed three men exit and make their way down the stairwell. She watched as they walked out, towards the car park. *No wonder there are more cars, that flat must be busy!* This did not sit well with her, she would be on the phone to David Young, as soon as she got into the office later.

Carol answered on the third chap of her door, "Oh Hi Vicki!" surprised to find her friend on the doorstep, "Come in, Charlie's here by the way..." sensing Carol's unease at her unexpected visit, "It's fine, If you'd rather I can come back later...I was only popping in to see how you were doing with the baby," Upon hearing who was the door, Charlie called, "It's all good Vicki, come on in!" Carol looked surprised and relieved, as she stepped back to allow Vicki access to the hallway. "Vicki has stopped by on her way to work, to see how I'm doing...that's nice of her, eh Babes?" Carol's nervousness at having the two of them together, was clear to see and hear. "Yeah, that was nice of her, take a seat," he replied, moving his feet from the settee. "It's okay I'm not staying long, I need to head to work soon," Vicki remained where she stood. "So, everything okay with you and the baby? Did you get a due date yet?" Carol lifted her top, to show off her baby bump, "All's good Vicki, we will have our baby in early June," Vicki could see how excited they both were at the prospect of becoming parents. "You ready for the sleepless nights Charlie?" she thought she should include him in their conversation, he was the Daddy after all. "Bleeding hell, I think he's practicing just now," laughed Carol, "Don't start Babe, I told you I've got a few things on my mind, that's all!" Charlie was quick to defuse Carol's worries. *Interesting!* Thought Vicki, he's obviously struggling to keep his act together! *Don't you even think about letting us down Charlie Sweeney! Too many people are depending on you!* Vicki looked directly at Charlie, "I'm sure everything will be fine, it will all go to plan!"

Chapter Thirty

Back at the office, David Young was already sitting waiting on Vicki coming into work. "Is she usually this late Dougie?" he had been waiting an hour and a half, he would need to be making his way to his own work soon. "Miss Carey works to her own hours at times, she should be due in soon", said Dougie, he was used to Vicki coming and going. This was not the kind of nine to five job people assumed it may be. There was a lot of investigating journalism done outside normal office hours, as long as her hours were made up, he did not mind. Five minutes later, Vicki entered the office, seeing them sitting in Dougie's office she walked straight over. "Hi, I hope you've not been waiting for me! The traffic was murder earlier, so I popped in to see Carol, find out how she was getting on." David was taken aback by how beautiful she looked this morning, he stopped himself from staring at her. *Maybe after all this is finished, she'll come out with me!* Momentarily side tracked he reminded himself of the reason for this visit. "Charlie Sweeney's been in touch again, with more information! We need to start acting on this info he's providing us with, before there are more bodies!"

Once David relayed the information, he had received earlier that morning, the three of them sat deep in thought, trying to come up with a plan, in order to prevent more unnecessary deaths. "Do you think maybe it is now time to bring in the Police? I mean the actual crime team!" Vicki was beginning to feel out of her depth. "The only thing stopping me from going to the crime team, is that, once they become involved, we will be put right out of the picture!" replied Dougie. "We have a lot to lose if we hand this over," it was the journalist in him, not wanting to let go of a good story. He realised the case was bigger than they had first assumed, he also had a responsibility regards his staff's safety, but his instincts were screaming at him, to hold on to it for the time being. "What's your thoughts David?" It was Vicki looking for reassurances from the professional in the room. "I say we give it another week working with Charlie, see what else he can tell us, then we hand all the information we have, over to the crime team!" he replied. He understood Dougie's reasoning for not wanting to bring the CID on board just now, but he also had a duty of care to the public, he was still an Officer after all!

Vicki spent the remainder of the day in the office writing up notes and filing. They had agreed to a plan of action, which involved putting Pete under surveillance. David had explained that Michael Gold was obviously using Pete to do his dirty work, moving and removing the young ones. Therefore, it made sense to keep an eye on him and record his every movement, hopefully prevent any more killings. David had left the office to go find their man Pete and start the surveillance. Once he had discovered where he was, he would keep in touch with Vicki and Dougie, Vicki would take over from David later in the day.

Part of the plan was for Vicki to keep in touch with Michael Gold. As far as they were concerned, he did not have any idea that they were on to him!

Lifting the telephone receiver, she noticed her hands shaking, she dialled his number. He answered quickly, "Hi Michael, it's Vicki," she was trying hard not to sound as nervous as she felt. "Oh Hello, I was wondering when I would hear from you again," a hint of surprise in his voice, "I was calling to thank you for the beautiful flowers, I have been so busy with my work, sorry it's taken me so long to get back to you!" she felt disgusted with herself, apologising to him, knowing what she knew of his business. "You're welcome, I'm glad you liked them, when I hadn't heard from you, I thought maybe roses were not your thing!" *He's playing with me here...*she struggled to keep her composure, she had to act nice to him. Acting interested in him romantically, was their only way in maintaining contact with him. When in reality, all she was wanting to do was scream at him and tell him how sick he made her feel! "What girl does not like roses?" she played along with him, "Ahh but you are not every girl Vicki...are you? You are special!" she felt physically sick. *Is this the way he talks to the young girls? Ugh! I hate you!* "Yeah, well thanks, I'll see you later," she did not want to listen to his voice any longer, "I'm sure you'll see me sooner than you think!" came his chilling reply, it sent shivers up her spine, as she replaced the receiver. *What the hell does he mean by that?* Vicki felt intimidated by him, not sure if it was because of the way he had spoken to her or if it was due to her knowing what he was really like now, she was less self-assured from when she had dialled his number.

Surveying Pete McNeil was turning into a busy full- time job!

Watching him exit from another tenement building, David looked on in disbelief, as he witnessed him direct two young girls and a boy into his car, then drive off. *You're a busy son of a gun! Where the hell are you taking these ones now?*

David had been given a list of addresses from Charlie, flats where he knew Pete visited on a regular basis. He caught up with Pete on Kilbarchan Road. David took in his surroundings with an air of caution, as it was a busy area of the Town which was notorious for trouble. There were old tenement buildings on either side of him, the occasional convenience store dotted here and there, a mix of nationalities catered for. It looked and felt a depressing place to stay, the feeling of danger and unrest was almost visible. He was busy taking in the many different people, when he noticed Pete's car sitting at the roadside outside a tenement building. Pulling up further along the road, David sat waiting to see if Pete was with someone or alone. He had not been sitting long when after ten minutes, Pete appeared with a young girl and two young boys. The young ones appeared dishevelled, it was there for the world to see. The girl wore a short mini-skirt and crop top, the boys had on shorts and crop tops. Knowing what he knew of their captivity, it was clear to see they had been force dressed, for sexual exploitation. *You piece of shit!* David felt sick to his stomach by what he had seen, it made him more determined to continue after Pete McNeil.

This was the third address, David had followed Pete McNeil to within the same area. He was surprised the flats were all so close in vicinity to each other, even more surprised that Pete felt safe moving the youngsters in broad daylight. David could not believe the way in which not one single person questioned this grown man with two vulnerable, scantily clothed teens. He did notice the majority of people walked either with heads low or looking straight ahead, he concluded that he wouldn't want to take in the views either. At every flat, Pete exchanged the young ones. David witnessed him enter with young people, spend around twenty minutes in the flat then leave with different young ones. *Interesting*! He soon realised he was watching the ring in action! Pete was moving the young people about like commodities, ensuring the punters never came into contact with the same one twice. The implications this must have on the young people was hard to imagine. *We need to stop this and soon*! David vowed to himself that he would do everything in his power to put an end to their suffering, as he watched the three young people being led into another flat, on the opposite side of the road, from where they had been removed from.

Chapter Thirty- One

As Vicki finished her work, she was pondering what she could grab for her dinner. Earlier she had arranged to meet David wherever he was, in his plight to follow Pete McNeil. *I'll stop at the chippy en route...*her stomach began rumbling at the thought of food. The sound of her telephone ringing on her desk brought her back to the moment. "Hello, Vicki Carey speaking," it was David, "Hi Vicki, meet me in the car park on the Elton, I've been all over this bloody town today, I'll explain when I see you, will you bring me some food please?" he said, matter of factly. Replacing the handset, she grabbed her coat and satchel then went on her way.

On arrival at the Elton Estate, she found David sat in his car with the heating on. "God, I'm freezing, I hope you have something hot to eat," almost grabbing the plastic carrier bag from her hands, as she entered his car. "Chippy...it should heat you up! I thought you were going to debrief me then head home?" puzzled by his actions. "Change of plan, after what I've witnessed today, I don't think it would be wise leaving you here yourself at night!" he stated. Curious, "Let's eat, then you can tell me everything."

Mixed emotions ran through Vicki when she heard all the details of David's day. One minute she felt rage, then sadness, then guilt, then back to rage! "I'll tell you this David, I will not rest until everyone of those pieces of scum are behind bars, for good! Who the hell do they think they are, using and abusing these kids?" David could see how angry she felt, her face was turning all shades of red, as she sat turning all the information over in her mind. "We will get them! We are already a good step ahead of them, let's wait and see if tonight shows us anymore..." he answered, trying to calm her down. Finished eating, David gulped down the last of his Coca Cola, collected the rubbish from around where they were sat. "Right! I'll be two minutes, I'm just going to put this in that bin over there." Vicki sat watching him walking towards the bin, he had discarded the rubbish and turned to return to the car, when she saw the car approach fast. Everything seemed to go into slow motion, as she watched the car speeding up ahead, straight in the direction of David. One minute he was on his feet then the next he was flying up in the air, as the car struck him! Vicki remained in the car, unable to move for a few seconds due the horror of what had just happened in front of her. Regaining her composure, she jumped out of the car and ran as fast she could, over to find David lying face down on the cold wet ground, with blood coming from his head. *OH MY GOD! OH MY GOD!*

"HELP! SOMEBODY HELP! PLEASE!!" she screamed, panic setting in. "David, hang in there, help is coming! Please be okay!" she cried, stroking his arm, as she looked around to see if anyone was coming to help them!

"I'll jump in for a bath, then we can watch that film which is on later…" she was looking forward to getting her shoes off and relaxing this evening. Charlie had turned up to walk her home from work. Recently, he had been surprising her by doing more things for her. Carol assumed it was because she was carrying his child, not that she was going to complain, she was enjoying spending more quality time together. Turning the corner to come onto the Estate, Charlie quickly grabbed Carol's sleeve to pull her backwards, as a car nearly ran them both over as it exited the Estate at speed. "Fecking idiot!" he called after the car, "Are you okay? That was close…" he stated, checking Carol was unhurt. "Yeah, I'm fine, just gave us a bit of a fright…Listen…Can you hear that? Someone shouting for help" she replied, walking in the direction in which she heard the cry for help.

"Look, Charlie…over there…someone's on the road, I bet it was that car which nearly hit us!" panic rising, Carol and Charlie ran towards the figures on the road. A small crowd was standing across from where a body lay on the ground, Carol could see the outline of a woman, bending over the figure on the road. "HURRY! PLEASE! SOMEONE CALL AN AMBULANCE!" Vicki was shouting at the crowd of people, which had appeared. "Someone's already calling them, they'll be here soon!" replied an older man. "Charlie quick…I think I recognise that voice…" closer now, Carol gasped in shock at the sight of Vicki, on her knees, crying trying to comfort the injured man on the ground. Running to help her friend, Carol eventually reached Vicki. Charlie was right behind her, "What happened Vicki? Are you okay? Are you hurt too?" she was panicking at the state her friend was in and the bloody covered man. Sobbing, Vicki lifted her tear stained face, to look past Carol and directly at Charlie, "This was not an accident! Someone was waiting to run us over!" Charlie stared straight ahead, unsure of what to say or do!

Chapter Thirty-two

Several hours passed, in which time David and Vicki were rushed to the Western Hospital. David was taken straight through to be assessed, whilst Vicki was escorted into a side room. The ambulance man had not given too much away, he was concerned by the fact that David had remained unconscious, he worked on him most of the journey to the hospital. Vicki had been examined on the scene, apart from being in shock, she was fine. Now she waited alone, in the room for the Police to come, ask her questions about the incident. *I hope to God he's going to be okay! If there is anyone up there listening, please make sure David comes through this...*Never, had she prayed as much, as she had done in the past few hours.

There came a knock at the room door, "Hello, we are looking for Miss Carey," two Police Officers, one male, one female. "Hi, that's me..." she replied, cautiously. "We understand you were with the victim at the time of the incident, if you wouldn't mind answering a few questions for us, in order to continue our enquiries," *SHIT! What am I going to say?* Anxiety building inside her, she was struggling to keep her composure, suddenly she burst out crying, tears streaming down her face. "Here, sit down." The female Officer took her by the arm and led her to a seat. "It must have been such a shock, to see PC Young taken down like that!" said the male Officer. "He only went to put the rubbish in the bin...the next minute he was in the air!" she was trembling, as the shock took hold of her body. "I think we had better get you home, we can talk again tomorrow," said the female Officer, as she helped Vicki to her feet, "Come with us, we will drop you off at your home."

"Mum! Mum!" she hollered, as she entered her house. Opening the living room door, her Mum hurried to her side, "What the bleeding hell is going on?" Vicki could see the shock and concern on her Mum's face. "Ohh Mum! it's been horrible!" the tears flooding from her eyes. "Come here," her Mum stopped her in her tracks, placed her arms around her and held her tightly. When the tears subsided, they both walked to Vicki's bedroom. "I think you need a lie down Vicks, I'll go make us both a nice cuppa, then you can tell me all about it!" Relaying the details in between sobs, Vicki managed to tell her Mum about the investigation, much to her Mum's horror, which was written across her face. "Jeezo, Vicki, it's terrible to think this is going on practically on our doorstep too, but you've placed yourself in real danger, you need to let the Police handle this from now on!" Vicki agreed with her Mum, "Don't worry Mum, I'll tell them everything we know, let them handle the rats."

The next morning Dougie could not believe what he was hearing, from the two Officers, that were standing in front of his desk. "So, you're telling me David was deliberately run over?" shaking his head in disbelief. "We are following up on more enquiries, so far from the statements we've collected, it's looking that way," explained the male Officer. "Can you tell us why he was on the estate in the first place?" asked the female Officer. "I think you had better take a seat..." replied Dougie, closing the door to his office.

As expected, the Officers were not happy at the information being withheld. Dougie tried his best to reassure them, that they were going to involve the Police, when the time was right. He promised to contact them later, once he had checked on Vicki, to ensure she was okay. When they eventually left the office, Dougie called Vicki at home, "Hi Vicki, how are you? I've already had the old bill here this morning, they told me what happened last night," she heard the concern in his voice. "I'm better than I was last night, it was awful Boss! Any news on David?" she intended checking up on him at the hospital, before going into work. "No news yet, but the old bill ain't happy with us Vicki, withholding information is a serious offence and they're wanting everything we have on the ring." He sounded defeated, "We will give them everything, in exchange for them allowing us to continue on the case..." There was no way she was handing over all the information for nothing., her future career depended on it!

Chapter Thirty-Three

Pete McNeil was a worried man.

Having escaped from the Elton flat undetected, he had taken refuge in Mick's flat, thinking it would be the last place anyone would look for him, since Mick was still unconscious in the hospital. He had no idea he was being followed, either by the copper or anyone else. He always checked behind him, in fact he felt that he spent most of his life looking over his shoulder, this fact alone was making his paranoia worse. Checking out of the window for the umpteenth time that morning, Pete's mind returned to the events at the Elton Estate once more. *How the hell did I miss someone following me? Who was the geezer that run the copper over?* Over and over in his mind, it was driving him insane. *Must've been the Gaffer, put someone on my tail...*Turning from the window, it suddenly hit him... *All this time I've been doing his dirty work and he's watching me...Fucker!* Anger building up inside him, he punched the wall, *Ouch!* Checking his knuckles for cuts, he walked towards the chair next to the fire, fell into it, put his head in his hands, trying to work out where he went from here!

Startled, he awoke from a deep sleep by the noise of the front door being chapped. Sitting upright, *Fuck! Who the hell's this?* Panic setting in, he tried to walk to the living room door as quietly as he possibly could. The front door was straight down the hallway and the top half was glass, he could make out the shapes on the opposite side of the door. *Looks like guys...*Realising they could be there looking for him, he got down on his knees, slowly and quietly, crawled to hide underneath the window. Crouched beneath the window he heard male voices outside, "There's no-one there! Place is empty...He's probably fled the country. Would you not, if you thought the Gaffer was onto to you?" followed by loud laughter, which sent chills up Pete's spine. *What the feck am I going to do?* He knew the last thing the Gaffer needed was attention, that he'd be unhappy about the situation on the Estate. Ultimately, he was being made the fall guy, the Gaffer would need to be seen to make an example of him! Waiting until the guys had left the street, Pete decided the only thing he could do was to ask Charlie for help, he was the only person he knew he could trust and was also caught up in this mess!

"Carol, here have another piece of cake..." offered Mrs Carey, "You need to keep your strength up you know, for you and the wee one," she pointed, towards Carol's extending baby bump. "Uch, I'm fine really, I only popped in for a quick cuppa, to see how Vicki was doing." She replied. "Stop fussing Mum, Carol can help herself to cake and biscuits," Vicki was fed up with her Mum fussing, since the accident she was non- stop. "Right then, I'll make myself scarce, leave you two in peace..." Vicki gave a sigh of relief, as she watched her Mum leave her bedroom. "Thank God, she's driving me insane," Carol gave a small laugh, "Yeah, but it's only natural Vicki, she's your Mum it's her job to worry and fuss, she probably got a fright as well," Vicki understood this. She had been instructed by Dougie to have a few days off, she was going stir crazy, sitting about drinking tea was not her idea of destressing. The only thing which she needed, was to be back working on the case and finding the guy that had run David over.

Lying on the settee, hands behind his head watching afternoon tv, Charlie was so relaxed he was nearly falling asleep. He had been relieved, when Carol had said she was going to pop into see Vicki. Ever since the incident on the Estate, she had not stopped talking about it, which was doing his head in! Charlie suspected it had something to do with the flat across the Estate. There was no way the copper had been run over as an accident, it was a message, which meant the Gaffer was onto something, which meant he was lying low and taking no chances.

Pete appearing at his door again, was the last thing Charlie wanted or needed.

Seeing the state Pete was in rattled Charlie's nerves. "What the hell is up with you?" he asked Pete, as they entered the living room. Pete was twitchy, there were beads of sweat on his forehead and upper lip. "Mate, you need to help me here..." Pete replied, going to the window and checking that no-one had followed him. "The Gaffer's got guys out looking for me, somehow I'm getting the blame for the other night, that copper getting run down...I mean I wasn't even in the fucking car," Charlie could see how anxious Pete was, which in turn worried him. "What do you mean, guys looking for you, how do you know?" he asked, as he sat on the settee. "There were guys at my flat asking if anyone had seen me, they've been to the Stag too, I got a message from the barmaid, telling me two guys were in asking questions about my whereabouts, so I went to Mick's place, thinking it would be last place they'd check, with him in the Western, but I've just come from there... they bloody well tracked me there," Charlie cut him off, "Right so you thought you'd come here...So they can trace you here now? Are you fecking daft?" Pete sat on the seat looking worried and rejected, "Charlie, I have nowhere else to go. If they get me, I'm a dead man, you know that as well as me, he's blaming me for the whole thing... it's not my fault!" Charlie understood what Pete was saying, but he had placed him in danger now by coming to his door. "Listen Mate, I hear what you're saying, but I cannot be getting involved in anymore shit! We've got a baby on the way, I need to be here to see it!" he declared, looking Pete straight in the eye. "Charlie, you are already involved in this, whether you like it or not, you are in this deep. If he comes for me, you can rest assure you'll be next!" Pete said, as he got up from his seat, he walked over to check out of the window again.

"What do you mean, you can't find him?" Michael Gold shouted, down the telephone line. "He's not Houdini, don't contact me again until you have him!" raging, he threw the receiver down, with a bang, then began pacing the office floor. *Fucking imbeciles! It's not hard to find someone, when you try! I'll probably end up finding him myself!*

Since the copper had been run down, Michael was under more pressure from the powers above him. They did not appreciate the attention which was now on the Estate, it was not good for their business. He had been contacted and told in no uncertain terms what would happen if he did not get it sorted. This meant that he would need to get rid of Pete McNeil, he was the one in charge of the area, it was his mistakes, which had led to being followed by the copper. If he had been more alert and on top of the game, this would not have happened. Michael would not allow one lazy man to bring down all he had worked so hard to build.

Chapter Thirty-Four

The sun was shining, and the first signs of spring were clear to be seen. Vicki loved Spring time it was her favourite season. The multicoloured crocuses and bright yellow of the daffodils beginning to show through, always made her feel optimistic and hopeful. Driving into work this morning she welcomed the sights and prayed this case would come to an end sooner rather than later.

Entering the office of The Daily, the first person she saw was Colin, "Your back Miss Carey...How are you doing?" he asked, checking her from head to toe. "Hello Colin, I am fine, thanks for asking, good to be back, did you miss me?" she was slightly taken back, he sounded sincere in his concern for her wellbeing. "It's just good to see you are still in one piece, now don't be going playing heroics again soon*!" There knew you couldn't be nice too long...*picking up on the sarcasm in Colin's voice. *Arsehole*! Giving him a small smile, she headed to Dougie's office for an update.

"So, we are not any further forward Boss?" Vicki was disappointed there had been no further leads on the **case**. "What about David, is he out of hospital yet?" she would go see him whether he was still in or at home recuperating. "He was discharged from hospital this morning, I don't know if he'll be up for visitors yet though," replied Dougie. Vicki had already decided she was going to see him, whether the Boss agreed or not. There was unfinished business which needed attending to right away!

Approaching the car park, as she left the office, Vicki had a feeling she was being watched. *Probably Dougie, watching from his office window.* Turning, looking up towards his window there was no sign of him there watching. *Maybe I'm imagining it,* she thought to herself, trying to shake off the feeling, she got in her car and drove to David's house on the edge of town.

As she drove along the street looking for the number of David's house, Vicki was pleasantly surprised by her surroundings. This was one of the new and upcoming areas, where new builds were suddenly popping up. The houses all looked similar, with light brown stonework and small patches of grass in front of bay windows. Most of the buildings were semi-detached houses, there was a block of flats further along the road. Eventually she found the number she was looking for, she smiled when she discovered it was a semi- detached house, in her mind she had David living in a manly bachelor flat.

It was David's Sister who opened the front door to his house. "Hi, my name's Vicki Carey, I've come to see David," she explained, "Oh, you were with him, when it happened, come in, come in," welcoming her inside to the hall. "He's not long settled, but I'm sure he'll be pleased to see you!" she continued, guiding Vicki to David's bedroom. When she saw him lying alone in his bed, she felt something stir inside herself, not for the first time. This had happened before, when she had come into contact with him, it had surprised her then just as much as it had taken her by surprise again today. Pushing her feelings aside, "Hello stranger, how are you feeling?" David blushed, pushing himself up into a sitting position, "Hi Vicki, nice of you to come see me, I'm a lot better than I was, if only this one here would stop fussing," laughing, he pointed towards his Sister. "Listen you gave us all a scare, you won't stop me fussing. Do you fancy a cuppa Vicki?" she asked, "That would be great, thanks," she replied. Once they were left alone in the room, "So what's the latest? Have the Police got any leads?" enquired Vicki. "They traced the car registration number, but it had been reported stolen, so nothing there," he sounded as disappointed as she felt at this news. "Rubbish...whoever it was must have been following you David, I mean how else would they know you were on the Estate, at that time?" raising her eyebrows, "I know it's been going round and round in my head, they must have caught on to me watching the flats and followed me from one..." Vicki agreed with him, it was the only answer she could think of as well. They spent an hour trying to piece everything they had together, "It's like a jigsaw isn't it? There are some bits missing, but rest assured we will get them David!" she reassured him, as she got up to leave, "Yeah, we will catch them, hopefully I'll be back to full fitness soon, but I'll be in touch when I hear from the Officers on the case," then she left, although, she would have been happier sitting in his company longer.

"Where are you taking all that food?" Carol called, watching Charlie bag sandwiches, soup and crisps into his rucksack. "Are you going somewhere without telling me?" she was getting worried, she had noticed things missing from the fridge and cupboards the past few days, but thought it was her mind playing games. "Babes, I've a friend in need, don't you go worrying your pretty head, all's good," he hoped this excuse would end her curiosity. "What friend?" *Awww for God's sake.* "Just a friend Babe, needs a bit of help with their food, you know he's skint, I'll replace everything later." Closing the bag, he grabbed his jacket, "See you later, I won't be long... love you!" then he was out the door fast. *He's bleeding well up to something, I know it*! Carol ran to the living room window, to see if she could find out where he was heading.

Running along the landing Charlie continually checked all around him, to see if there was anyone watching him. Down the stairwell, onto the Estate, he looked up to find Carol watching him from their living room window. *Fucking woman! Give it a rest!* He was already nervous, the last thing he needed was Carol adding to it. Taking a deep breath, he decided he would deal with her questions later, she was nothing compared to what he was dealing with. Giving her a wave, she waved back then disappeared from the window. *Thank Fuck!* Releasing a big sigh, he continued, to make his delivery.

Knocking at the door eight times, Pete knew it was Charlie. They had arranged for him to stay in one of the empty flats on the Estate. Charlie was the one to come up with the idea of hiding him in plain sight. It had taken a lot of encouragement to get Pete to finally agree to hiding out on the Estate. Charlie had explained it would be the last place they would be expecting to find him...right under their noses! They had found the empty flat late one night, they had checked a few ones they had knowledge of, they decided on this one, as it had less damp than the rest and appeared cleaner. They had moved during the night, making it comfortable with household bedding, a kettle and a microwave oven, which Charlie had brought from Mick's place. They assumed this was going to be Pete's hideaway for a long time, or until Michael Gold and his men were under lock and key.

Pete unlocked the door, Charlie pushed it open then stepped over the threshold. The first thing Charlie noticed was how unkempt Pete was looking. He did not have the luxury of personal grooming products, he was looking and smelling more like a vagabond everytime he visited him. "Mate, we'll need to get you deodorant, get a wash, the taps work you know..." Charlie remarked jokingly, although he was serious. Pete was already in a bad way, he did not want to make him worse. "I'll try sneak some out when the missus isn't watching, she already thinks I'm up to something, bloody murder Mate!" shaking his head, Charlie was dreading having to go home to face Carol's questions. Pete laughed, "Something I ain't missing here...a nagging woman. Did you make sure no-one followed you?" It was clear to see how anxious the situation was making Pete, "Did my best Mate, I need to talk to you about an idea..." Pete frowned, "If it's going to get me out of this then I'm all ears..."

Chapter Thirty-Five

Having spent the afternoon in the office going through all the paperwork for the investigation, she had made the decision to continue the surveillance on the estate on her own. She tried justifying it to herself, *If I remain in my car, then nothing can happen to me!* Feeling empowered, she left the office to grab a bite to eat, before heading off to the Elton for the evening.

Parking her car at the side of the car park, she turned off the engine before reaching across to the passenger side for her chippy tea. *May as well get comfortable...*she told herself, pulling her seat back from the steering wheel to stretch her legs. It was dark outside, the overhead lighting from the street lamps, was the only help she had, as she watched people coming and going. Earlier, she had felt as though someone was watching again, but she put it down to paranoia for being back on the Estate again. *Place gives me the creeps...*she could never stay in a place like this. Having grown up in a house with a garden, she never really appreciated it until her work brought her to this Estate. Looking closely at the people's faces, as they passed by her car, most of them looked so unhappy, with the weight of the world upon their shoulders. Finished eating, she was just about to open her car door to go put the rubbish in the bin, suddenly fear gripped at her.

Driving onto the Estate was Michael Gold!

Shit! Shit! Shit! Feeling her heart beat faster, she was certain he could hear it too! *What the hell am I going to do now?* Sliding down in her seat, trying to maintain a view of his car, she witnessed him signal to another driver in a car on the opposite side of the car park. He flashed his lights once and they flashed back. *I wasn't imagining being watched! Maybe it's not me they are watching.* A sense of calm came over her, as she watched Michael's car drive off the Estate again. Remaining where she was, she tried to identify the driver of the other car, which was still parked opposite. *No...don't think I know him*; her eyes grew sore from the intensity of her glare. It was apparent the more she watched him, that he was not watching her, as he did not look in her direction once. He appeared to be watching the flat, from where she had freed Mandy and where Michael Gold had visited. *I wonder if there are girls still in there...there must be, why else would he be guarding the flat?*

Driving away from the Estate, Michael was enraged at what he had just witnessed. *Does she honestly think I'm that bloody stupid?* Banging his fist off the steering wheel, he made his way back along the motorway in the direction of his house. There was no way he could get to the flats, to check if the information he had been given regards Pete McNeil's whereabouts, was true or not with her being present on the Estate. *Damn woman! Why can't you just leave things alone?* Frustration mounting within him, he was becoming angrier, thinking of Vicki and the situation, they now found themselves in. *As if it's not bad enough with that clown Pete, she's lending herself to my problems as well...* Pressure building up in his head, Michael looked away from the road, as he rubbed at his forehead, suddenly the car veered from the lane he was in, headed straight into the grass verge off the motorway, turning onto its side...Vicki's face, being the last image he saw!

*I'll give it another half hour, then I'm calling it a night...*thought Vicki, as she sat in her car watching people come and go on the Estate. It had been at least an hour, since she had seen Michael drive through and there had not been anything suspect since. Sitting in this confined space was not doing her any good, she had lost the feeling in her bum and she was getting cramps in her legs. *Maybe I should get out and walk about a bit, try get my circulation going again...*Slowly, she opened the car door, she looked about nervously, taking in her surroundings with fresh eyes. *Perhaps this isn't the best idea....* Now that she was out in the open, all she could see were the dangers. The lack of lighting, the emptiness of the Estate, her anxiety and paranoia, a mix which was not helping her maintain a clear head. Looking up at the many doors which surrounded her, she could hear some open and closing, yet there was no-one to be seen. Slowly, she began walking in and out the other parked cars which were plentiful, ensuring to stay well clear of the area where she had witnessed the car flash its lights to Michael. Feeling the cold night air on her skin, she decided to return to her car and head home. As she turned the key in the ignition, she revved the engine once and the radio came on. Vicki did not drive off, instead her attention had been drawn to the story the reporter on the radio was telling. Listening intently, she sat unable to believe what she was hearing, *I'm one hundred percent sure that's the make and model Michael Gold was driving earlier, that would've been about the same time too...* thinking this was too much of a coincidence.

Chapter Thirty-Six

The glimmer of morning light through her bedroom curtains awoke Vicki the next day. Feeling exhausted from a sleepless night, she turned over in her bed and pulled the duvet cover over her head. Throughout the night, she felt as though she had seen every minute change on the alarm clock by her bedside table. Mixed emotions and thoughts had whizzed around in her head all night, ensuring she had little to no sleep. Turning onto her back, she lay wrapped in her duvet and stared at the ceiling. The only solution in moving forward, which she kept going back to, was the fact that she needed David back on his feet and back working alongside her, she could not and did not, want to be left alone to bring justice for the trafficked youngsters. Mustering all the energy she could find from within, she got out of her bed, looked out her fresh clothing and headed to the shower. *Right girl! let's get them!* Adrenalin coursing through her veins once more...

"Hey Babes, it's your turn to make the tea," Carol called from the bathroom. Charlie was lying awake, although he had yet to open his eyes to welcome the new day. *Maybe if I lie like this long enough, I'll fall asleep...* he tried convincing himself. The pressure of providing information to the copper and keeping Pete hidden was seriously affecting him. The amount of sleep he was losing, was beginning to show on him, both mentally and physically, to the point he was not sure how much more he could take. Slowly, opening his eyes to the morning light, he vowed he would try his best to bring an end to this business and hopefully get some normality back into his life. Automatically, when he thought of a normal life, his mind would envisage the image of Carol, himself and their baby. This image always energised him, he was excited, for the upcoming birth and what the future would bring the three of them together. "You out of bed yet?" came Carol's dulcet tones, he jumped out of the bed, as he heard her clomping down the hallway in his direction. "Just on my way Babes, two ticks and I'll have your cuppa ready," he reassured her, giving her a kiss on the cheek, as he passed her on his way towards the kitchen. Carol looked beautiful to him all the time, today as he looked at her standing in front of him, he had to admit, she suited being pregnant. She had a glow about her. Upon entering the kitchen, he turned the radio on, before filling the kettle with water at the kitchen sink. He froze on the spot, turning the running water off, when he heard the latest local news from the radio station. Apparently, there had been a bad accident on the motorway, which had resulted in the death of a man they could now identify, as one Michael Gold!

Surely it couldn't be the same one...

Every morning driving into work, Vicki had to go along a stretch of motorway, however, this morning she was more interested in this part of her drive due to the road accident, which she had heard about on the radio last night. It was coming up to the next news round on the radio, she turned the volume up, not wanting to miss any details they might give, regards the driver's identity. On the dot of eight, the newsreader broke the news of the road accident on the motorway, **"Around eight pm last night, the emergency services were called to reports of a car, which had suddenly veered off the road close to Junction 14 of the motorway. The vehicle left the road directly onto the grassy verge, where it then rolled down the verge several times, resulting in the death of the male driver. He has been identified, as Michael Gold, who originated from the Hollowburn area, there were no other casualties."** Vicki's heart dropped, unsure if she had heard correctly or if her ears were playing games with her. *OH MY GOD! It can't be true...*Aware she was in shock, she drove as carefully as she could along the motorway. Passing the scene of the accident, she, could see some leftover remnants, from the emergency services, on the other side of the central reservation.

Parking the car in the designated area, Vicki could not remember her drive or how she had made it to work in one piece. It was all a blur, from the moment she had heard Michael's name on the radio, shock ran through her body. "Vicki, You're here!" It was Dougie, walking across the office area to meet her, as she entered. "I take it you've heard the news...about the accident last night?" His question was answered when she nodded her head, as tears fell from her eyes. Placing his arm gently around her shoulders, he escorted her through to his office for some privacy. "Here, sit down, I'll make us a strong cuppa," he stated, looking at Vicki in this state, he questioned whether he had done the right thing, allowing her to carry on with the investigation.

Vicki could not stop crying. This whole investigation was one big nightmare, she wasn't sure where to go from here. Dougie returned with two cups of steaming hot tea, "Need to let it cool a bit," he told her, placing the cups on the desk in front of her. "Do you think David will know?" she asked in between sobs. "I'm sure he will have heard by now... we can give him a call, once you're more settled." Opening his desk drawer, Dougie found a packet of tissues and offered them to her. Vicki accepted the tissues, opened them and blew her nose. Taking a deep breathe, she proceeded to tell Dougie about her last sighting of Michael. "I must have been one of the last people to see him alive, well apart from whoever was in the other car he flashed at..." blinking hard, she tried her best to hold back more tears. Eventually, her tears subsided, she drank the warm tea and sat back in her chair. "This whole thing is a nightmare Boss!" Dougie seated across from her nodded in agreement, "It has certainly gone off in directions which none of us were expecting, that's for sure, I think we should call David now, if you feel up to it?" Vicki nodded in agreement, as Dougie dialled his number, she sat patiently, hoping and praying that David was close to making a full recovery, she needed him!

Chapter Thirty-Seven

As expected, the news of Michael Gold's sudden death spread across the Town like wild fire. Some people were saddened. However, the majority of people were delighted and relieved. It differed, in accordance to which Michael Gold people had come into contact with.

Charlie, upon hearing the news from the radio could not contain his delight at the demise of his and Pete's tormentor. Once he had made the breakfast, he had rushed over to the safe flat where Pete was hiding. Knocking on the door eight times, he waited excitedly, he could not wait to tell Pete the news. He hoped the Gaffer being dead would mean the end of their problems. Eventually, Pete answered the door, looking worse than he had the day before. *This good news has come at the right time*, thought Charlie, taking a big lungful of fresh air, before stepping into the smelly flat. "Have I got news for you Pete! This is going to ease your troubles and mine..." Pete stood looking at him, with a puzzled expression on his face. "What the bleeding hell you on about?" Charlie could not contain the news any longer, "The Gaffer's dead Pete! DEAD! His car went off the motorway, rolled a few times, he didn't get out alive..." Charlie saw the shock on Pete's face, as he tried to digest the information, he had just been given. "Are you sure it's the same Michael Gold? There might be a few in the world, I don't suppose he's the only one..." Pete was struggling to take this in and what it would mean for them now. "It is THE same one! There was a picture of him on the news this morning, because he was known in the criminal world, it deemed news worthy." Charlie had switched the television on, after he had heard the news on the radio earlier that morning, for the exact same reason Pete was sceptical, he had to be certain himself. Both men made their way into the living room, sat down and discussed what this news meant for them and their situation.

Days later, making her way towards David's house, Vicki had a flutter in her stomach and an eagerness to see him again. When Dougie had called to ensure he had heard the news regards Michael Gold's untimely death, she was overjoyed to hear him say he was feeling better and fit enough to join them back on the case. The only problem was that he was not able to drive, due to his leg injuries not being one hundred percent healed, but other than that, he was ready to join them once again. Vicki reassured him she had no difficulty in being his chauffeur, she was looking forward to spending more time with him. Turning the corner onto the street where he lived, she pulled up outside his house and peeped her car horn to let him know she had arrived. Within seconds David was out the house, she watched as he locked the door, then turning, he slowly made his way towards her car. "God... it's so good to see you out and about again," she meant every word. "It feels good being back in the world of the living Vicki, I don't think I could've stayed locked up much longer," he turned to look at her, they both laughed together in agreement, as she drove off. "I got a phone call from Charlie Sweeney the night before Michael Gold had his accident. He was keen to meet up, as soon as possible, said he had more info and someone he wanted me to meet. I think we should start with giving him a visit, see what he's got for us...eh?" Vicki agreed, "The only thing is...How are we going to get to see him? What if that guy is still watching the Estate? We are going to have to be careful...I don't think we need anymore casualties, do we?" she asked, looking over in his direction. The rest of the drive to the Elton Estate went quickly, as they derived a way in which they could reach Charlie safely.

Outside the rain was falling heavily, it was dull and grey, *What a fecking depressing day it is*...thought Charlie, checking out of the living room window. Charlie looked across at the flat where he knew two girls remained. *I wonder what's going to happen now, with the big Gaffer out of the picture.* He had noticed a few guys still going in and out of the flat, but he did not know who they were, as he had never come across them before. Just as he was about to turn and walk away from the window, a female figure walked past on the landing, the next thing he knew, Vicki Carey was standing outside his door. *What the bleeding hell does she want*...Charlie tried to ignore the persistent chapping of the door. "I'm coming, hold your horses!" he shouted, walking down the hallway to open the door. "What?" was all he could muster for this unwelcome visitor, "If you're looking for Carol, she's at Tracey's" he told her, peering from behind the door, counting the minutes until he shut it in her face. Although they behaved amicably in front of Carol, neither Vicki or himself had moved forward in their thinking of each other. "I've actually come to see you, it's about the telephone call you made to PC Young the other night..." Vicki realised she needed to be as direct with him as possible, if she were to get his attention. It was clear to see the look of surprise of on his face, even though he was trying to disguise it, she noticed the twitch of realisation. "You had better come in then, I'm not talking to you here!" Charlie opened the door fully now, stood back to let allow his nemesis access.

Vicki felt strangely awkward, being in Carol's flat, without her being there. Taking a seat on the couch, she was aware Charlie did not want her there either, but she shrugged of the feeling of unease. *There are more important things at stake right now, than our feelings...* "So... what is the new information you have?" she knew time was not on their side. The fact Michael Gold was out of the picture now did not in any way mean the trafficking had stopped. The Romanian gang would not stop due to his untimely death, there would always be someone else to take his place. David had explained to her on the drive over to the Estate that the Police were aware of another young girl's body, which had been discovered after the death of Michael Gold. Charlie smirked at her, "Do you seriously expect me to sit here and tell YOU!" looking at her bemusedly. "Charlie, I realise we will never get on and that we have to put on a show for Carol's sake, but there are bigger issues here, which need dealt with! David Young and I are looking at this sex trafficking ring together, for obvious reasons we thought you would understand, it's safer for me to be seen coming to your door, than him, given that the flats were being watched, you choose!"

Who the Feck does she think she's talking to? Charlie sat glaring at Vicki across the room from him. "If I told you that another young girl's body has been discovered, would that help make up your mind?" Vicki was beginning to think he was not going to tell her anything, she needed to get him on their side and fast. Charlie was shocked to hear this, he realised the Romanians would not stop because of the Gaffer's death, yet, the news they had killed again made him fear for Pete and himself once more. "Alright I'll tell you everything I know, but I've got a mate who can tell you much more detail than I can! We need to go speak to him, I've had to hide him because the Gaffer was onto him after the copper got run over, blamed Pete for bringing him onto the Estate..." *Bingo...*Upon hearing the name Pete, the adrenalin began rushing through Vicki, she recognised the name as one Mandy had mentioned. *If this is the same person, this could be massive intelligence wise...* Firstly, they had to ensure they got to him, before the Romanians did!

Downstairs waiting in Vicki's car David watched, as two big burly looking guys got out of a black Mercedes, proceeding towards the first stairwell. *This is getting interesting, hopefully Vicki won't meet these two on the stairs...* The rain continued to fall heavily, this was not making it easy to keep a watchful eye on the two men. David rolled down the car window in order to help make it easier to watch for himself. Moments passed, then suddenly he noticed them, walking along the landing of flat number six. *Jesus, I hope they're not going up there to cause those girl's more harm, hurry up Vicki...*

Chapter Thirty-Eight

Meanwhile, Vicki and Charlie were, for once, placing their differences aside and trying to come up with a safe plan to reach Pete McNeil, without bringing any unwanted attention their way. The air within the living room was thick with apprehension, "If you go to the flat first, knock eight times, he'll come to the door, thinking it's me," Charlie suggested, "Then once he's answered, tell him I sent you and give him the coppers' name...he'll let you in then," Vicki was not sure how she felt about going into a flat alone with this guy Pete, given all that she already knew of him. *I'll get David to come with me, I don't want to go alone...*recognising the fear she was feeling inside, as she sat listening to Charlie's idea.

Outside the rain had subsided slightly, making it easier for David to oversee the flats. *Where the hell are you Vicki?* Time had passed so slowly, since he had seen the two guys enter number six, anticipation and his mind visualising all sorts of untoward things going on, was driving him insane. *If you're not back here in ten minutes, I'm coming looking...*he promised himself, looking up at the landings once more.

"Right, so you know what you need to do?" Charlie was feeling nervous about letting Vicki go to the flat alone, they had decided this was the only option, until they were certain the flats were not being watched, but it was not sitting easy with him. Having spent time with her, just the two of them, he realised she wasn't as bad as he had first thought. He'd come to the conclusion, when this was all over, he might even come to like her, she was smart, nothing appeared to scare her, qualities he admired in a woman. "Yeah...Yeah... everything else you've told me I have written in my notes, you realise you will still have to talk to the Police, make a statement..." The information Charlie had provided her with was good and would help them, he had explained his involvement and assured her that Pete could provide all the details to bring down the ring. Physically, Vicki felt sick and overwhelmed with the enormity of the task in hand.

Making her way out of Carol's flat onto the landing, Vicki looked across at flat number six, then down to the car park to see whether she could identify whether the landings were under surveillance or not. *Shit!* Sitting in the car park she noticed the black Mercedes, straining her eyes to see inside, she realised the car was empty. *Feck! Means they're out here somewhere...* Quickly, she glanced across then down again, before heading off to find Pete McNeil.

Time's up Vicki! I'm coming to find you... David left the safety and comfort of the car behind him, running across the Estate carpark to escape the rain. Entering the first stairwell his nose was accosted by the usual smell of urine and the sight of graffiti. Heading in the direction of Carol's flat, he made it to the top of the stairs, onto the landing, his eye was drawn across from where he stood...*Bloody hell...* he could not believe what he was seeing!

Across the Estate Vicki had just finished climbing up her third set of stairs, puffing and panting, *Oh my God, these bloody stairs are going to kill me...* Stopping to catch her breath, she checked the landing ahead of her, *Fourth door along, that's what he said...* Taking a deep breath to try steady herself, Vicki set off along the landing. As she made her way towards the door, she casually looked across to the opposite landing, what she saw stopped her in her tracks. *Shit!* Without thinking, she turned, running back along the landing, taking the stairs two at a time, until she reached the bottom. Once there, she ran from the stairwell towards her car, panic set in when she saw her car was empty. *David! Where the bloody hell are you? Feck sake!* Standing next to her car, she scanned the car park in-case he was stretching his legs, no sight of him. Suddenly, she heard footsteps and a male voice speaking in a threatening manner. *Romanians...* One of the young girls they were dragging along was crying, "SHUT UP!" shouted one of the men, slapping the girl behind her head. *You fecker!* Vicki sent up a silent prayer, adrenalin took over, she stepped out from behind a car, "HEY!" she called loudly, "OVER HERE!" she called again, to get the attention of the men. *OH SHIT! They've stopped!* Further along from where she stood, the men had pulled the girls to a sudden stop. Slowly, they turned to face her!

From the upper landing, David was watching as the two men and young girls, appeared from the stairwell across from where he stood. *I don't bloody believe* *this...They obviously think they're untouchable, dragging them like that in broad daylight...*Shaking his head, he stopped in disbelief, he then recognised Vicki standing at the side of her car. *OH NO! Stay there Vicki, do not move...*hoping she would not do anything stupid. Moving as fast as his injured leg would allow, David was in agony by the time he exited the stairwell onto the Estate. The next thing he heard was the sound of Vicki's voice.

Chapter Thirty-Nine

Watching from his window Charlie was stunned at what he was seeing. At the sight of the two big Romanians hauling the small girls from the flat, he worried that they might cross paths with Vicki on the stairwell. Grabbing his jacket, Charlie ran as fast as he could along the landing, jumping down most of the stairs, until he reached the bottom. Deciding to hide himself from sight, he crouched down in between two parked cars and waited. *I think I've beaten them...* he slowed down his breathing and waited. Crying and footsteps were the first signs Charlie heard, telling him he had made it onto the Estate before them. *Shit! They look petrified...poor kids...* When he witnessed one of the big guys swearing and slapping a girl behind her head, he ran from his place of safety, out into the open space of the car park, towards the girls.

"HEY!"

Who the feck was that? Turning his head from side to side, he was surprised to find Vicki walk from behind some parked cars. As she shouted again, "OVER HERE!" he noticed the party in front stop, turning to face them both now. *What the fecking hell is she playing at?* Fear hitting him now, standing in front of the Romanians, they glared at him, as the adrenalin left his body. *We are feckin dead...*

Seeing Charlie there made Vicki feel surprisingly confident. Standing in front of the Romanians, she felt a rush of energy, "LEAVE THOSE GIRLS ALONE!" amazing herself, she stood her ground. One of the Romanians let out a laugh, replying in broken English he asked, "AND YOU ARE...WHO?" as he moved forwards. *You're not going to scare me, you fecker!* At this point, she felt so angry at all the injustices, which this gang were benefitting from, she thought of Mandy and the poor girls who did not make it. Taking a step forward, she waited to see what his next move was going to be.

"VICKI! STOP!" It was Charlie calling across to her. "YES! LISTEN TO YOUR FRIEND!" called the Romanian. Vicki stood still, looking from Charlie to the Romanians and back again. Suddenly, she realised the scenario she was caught up in now. Fuelled by anger, she replied," LET THE GIRLS GO FREE...THAT'S ALL WE WANT!" Laughing loudly, the Romanian pulled a gun from inside his jacket. "YOU THINK YOU ARE GIVING THE ORDERS?" menacingly, waving the gun in the air. At the sight of the gun Vicki felt her knees go weak, *OH FECK!*

David watched in horror at the scene unfolding in front of him. Assessing the situation quickly, he crouched down and made his way as close to where Vicki was standing as possible. *Vicki please shut up!* He silently pleaded with her, hoping somehow, she would receive his message. He thought Vicki was smarter than to place herself in this kind of danger. The sight of the Romanian walking towards her sent shivers down his spine when he heard him mocking her, he feared for her life. *Please, just shut up and walk away Vicki...Walk away!*

"WAIT!" shouted Charlie, slowly walking in the direction of the Romanian. "STOP WHERE YOU ARE!" he replied, pointing the gun directly at him. *Feck! This guy's going to pull that trigger...* Charlie was scared, for once in his life he had a future to look forward to with Carol and the baby, now he was going to die, he'd never see his baby! "PLEASE, JUST TURN AMD WALK AWAY, SHE DOESN'T KNOW WHAT SHE'S SAYING...PLEASE!" he realised he was begging for his life, but he did not care... if it meant he'd get to live. The Romanian turned from Vicki, he was now pointing the gun directly at Charlie. *OH NO!* Before she had time to think, instinct took over...Vicki turned, she began running towards Charlie.

BANG! BANG!

Chapter Forty

It was a beautiful summer day, the sun was shining bright in the clear blue sky, it was good to feel the heat on her skin, as she pushed the pram along in the park. Today, she had agreed to meet David Young. *Looks like him over there...God he looks awful!* He looked up at her and waved. "Hi David, nice to see you again," she placed the brake on the pram and sat down alongside him on the bench. "Hi, lovely day for a walk in the park," Carol had only met him a handful of times, the last time being at the funeral, she felt awkward and unsure of what to say to him.

Just then the baby began to cry...

"Would you mind if we walked a little, she seems to like it better when I'm on the move, hates letting me sit for two minutes," she gave a little laugh, trying to lighten the mood. David agreed and stood up, "That's babies for you, made to keep Mum busy!" smiling, he looked in the pram. "Does she have a name yet?" Carol felt apprehensive, she was not sure how he would take her reply. "Mmm...Yeah we called her Zoe...Zoe Victoria Sweeney..." she noticed the change in him, as soon as she had mentioned her name!

All around them was bright, the beautiful trees were all different shades of green, a variety of brightly coloured flowers were in full bloom and children were running around playing. Yet, where they walked Carol felt the tension, as though a large black cloud was above them. *Jeezo, why did I agree to this, I should have stayed away...* Carol felt bad for David, although they had all struggled since the shooting, he appeared to be taking it really bad, Carol assumed it was because he had feelings for Vicki. "It's a lovely name for a lovely baby," he replied eventually. "Well, we thought it only fitting that she has Vicki's name in there...all things considered she's a bit of a heroine in our house!" she stated. David nodded his head slowly, in agreeance.

"I only wish I had moved faster, tried stopping her, before...you know..." Carol could almost see the guilt and sadness, he held within himself. "David it's not your fault, there was nothing you could do, or anyone for that matter. Once Vicki made her mind up about something, well, that was that...No-one could've stopped her! Vicki was set on getting that story and freeing those young people. I'm sorry she did not get the chance to see her name in the big National papers...she would have loved that!" Carol knew first hand, from past experience, once Vicki set her sights on a goal, there was no point trying to talk her out of it, she simply would not listen.

"Charlie has been feeling the same!"

Since the shooting, the months had passed, yet for the ones involved, it felt like it had all happened only yesterday...

As the Romanian fired the gun in Charlie's direction, Vicki had run straight into the path of the first bullet. Time stood still... Everyone watched in horror, as she fell to the ground, holding her blood covered stomach. Charlie threw himself to the ground to try and cover her, but the second bullet had already hit her! David had run, from in between the parked cars, when he had seen Vicki run, but he was too late! Vicki lay helpless on the ground, whilst Charlie tried to stem the blood, which was pouring from her fast, the bullet had cut through a main blood vessel, there was nothing they could do to save her! The Romanians had quickly fled the scene, leaving the two girls behind. When David had eventually realised, they were running, he quickly made a note of their car registration, before running back across to where Vicki and Charlie lay. The rest of the night went by in a blur, for all involved. The ambulance had arrived quickly, but not fast enough for Vicki, she was pronounced dead at the scene. Charlie, David and the two young girls were all treated for shock at the scene, before being transferred to the hospital for further checks.

The first Carol became aware of an incident on the Estate, was when she had answered the door to the Police. When they had explained there had been a fatal shooting and Charlie was involved, she fainted! The Officers had managed to bring her around, but they thought she would be better getting checked over by a Doctor, just to be safe, giving that she was expecting a baby. When Charlie heard that Carol was in the hospital he rushed to be by her side. As he walked into the cubicle, where she lay on the bed, Carol looked up at him, then burst into tears. Apologising over and over again, Charlie held her in his arms, trying to calm and comfort her.

Eventually, they were discharged from the hospital and allowed home. Carol did not want to go back to the Estate straight away, all she could think about was Vicki lying bleeding to death in the car park, she could not cope with being around all the commotion, Charlie took her to Tracey's instead. There were things he needed to tell her...

David had gone straight home once he had been discharged from the hospital. Closing his front door behind him, he had sunk to his knees, held his head in his hands and cried, like he had never cried before. The frustration from the case had been building up inside of him, the enormity of the trafficking ring had made him feel helpless, as an Officer. He knew deep down the ring would never be fully stopped, all he could hope for was that it was brought to an end and prevented from growing further in his area. Still, as the tears fell, he knew they were because of Vicki! He had known for some time he had feelings for her, as they had spent more and more time together, the feelings had become stronger. There had been times, when they had been together, he would have sworn she felt the same. Now he would never know... He continued crying further into the night for the love he had lost...

The two young girls were released into the care of Social Work. It became evident that they had been brought to England in the back of lorry, on the promise of cleaning and looking after small children, Once, they had arrived they were taken to a flat and introduced into paying for their keep by using their bodies. Both girls had been terrified, but could not find a way out, as they were under lock and key, only seeing the light of day when they were being moved to a new flat. Through interpreters, they were able to provide the Police with more information regarding the Romanians. So far, they had arrested four Romanian men and Pete McNeil...

Charlie was sickened at the events which had taken place. After telling Carol of his involvement with the gang and becoming an informer, they decided he had to go to the Police to tell them everything which he knew, if they were to have a future together... as a family unit. With a mix of emotions Charlie had gone to the Police Station and told them everything, including the whereabouts of Pete. Due to him helping with the investigation, he was told he may still face a prison sentence. Unfortunately, Pete's change of heart to help the coppers had come too late. After Charlie had divulged all the gory details, including the death of three young girls, the Police had to arrest him for their murders, once the trafficking was added, Pete would be locked up for a long time. However, as far as Charlie was concerned, they would do their best to try to keep him out of jail. All he could now was wait...

Having promised to keep in touch, Carol left David at the park gates, to walk home to the Estate. "Carol! Wait up!" turning, she saw Charlie running towards her. "Where have you been?" she asked curiously, since he had told her about his involvement with the gang, she did not totally trust him, it was going to take time to gain her trust back in him, if she ever could. "I called in on Mary and Peter, showed them the baby pictures, they're looking forward to getting a cuddle..." It was important to him that they both played a part in his family life, after all they were his family! "Aww that's nice, yeah you should invite them over for tea," Carol knew how important it was for Mary and Peter to see him with his own family. Laughing, he replied, "Glad you said that Babe, I've asked them over next week, that's okay?" Carol rolled her eyes in reply, before holding out the pram to allow Charlie to take over from pushing it. Together, they walked along deep in their own thoughts. Charlie broke the silence first, "You know, it's weird how life works out sometimes...ain't it?" Carol nodded her head, unsure where he was going with this train of thought, "Yeah, I suppose it does...Anything in particular?" Charlie glanced over at her, "Well...Take You and me...We wouldn't have met way back yonder if it hadn't been for Mary and Peter...OR dare I say it, Vicki!" Carol looked across at him, sometimes he took her by surprise, now was one of them, "That's deep coming from you," laughing, nervously, "It's not like you to give credit to anyone, especially Vicki..." Charlie stopped walking, turned to look directly at her, "Now Carol, that's not true! If it wasn't for Vicki, I might not be here at all...I mean alive! For all we had our moments, I think we were growing on one another..." he checked, to see whether she was agreeing with him, "I'd say more than growing, she tried to save you, for whatever reason, she put herself in harms way for you!" To this day. Carol struggled to find a reason why Vicki had put herself in front of Charlie. "That's what Mary was talking about today, she told me Vicki had sanctified herself!" Looking up, into the face of the man she loved with all her heart, Carol leant in and kissed him on the cheek, "I think Mary might be right Charlie!" placing her arm through his, they walked the rest of the journey home in silence. Each one lost in their own thoughts of their friend Vicki. Grateful for each other, their baby daughter and the future they had ahead of them, together. A FAMILY!

THE END

A WORD FROM THE AUTHOR

I hope you have enjoyed reading this book.

It has been three years since my first novel No Sanctuary was published. The idea for this book came one night and I began to plan and write a few months after my first release. It has taken me longer than expected to reach this point of publication. In the past three years my family and I have experienced some of the horrible aspects of the life cycle, with the loss of some loved ones.

I'm sorry to my readers for the delay on this book. I thank you from the bottom of my heart for your patience and continued support, it is very much appreciated!

A special mention to my two Besties, for the love, support and understanding they have shown. Always there to listen to me ranting, when writing is not going to plan and encouraging me on!

I would like to give a VERY big THANK YOU, to my Other Half, Son and Hannah, also Charlie (my furbaby) for all of their support and unconditional love! Encouraging me when I felt unsure, even providing me with some ideas. Putting up with me working away into the small hours of the night, bringing endless supplies of coffee and sweets throughout the days, ensuring I was fed whilst I worked. Charlie keeping me company, never leaving my side providing me with all the cuddles I needed! I'm blessed with my wee family, at the end of the day, FAMILY is ALL we NEED!

Dedicated
in
Memory of
May & Bert

Always and Forever

WE ARE ALL STARS WRAPPED IN SKIN –
THE LIGHT YOU ARE SEEKIN

HAS ALWAYS BEEN WITHIN!